trying to cling to one another through the storms of war. Sensitively told, with a mixed Chinese-American family at its heart, *Dragonfly Dreams* draws young readers towards perhaps their first inkling of this particular abyss with a light touch and empathetic heart."

—MELISSA FAY GREENE, author of *Praying for Sheetrock* and *The Temple Bombing*

"Focusing on a young Chinese-American girl named Nini, whose life is suddenly turned upside down by the takeover of her hometown in northern China by the Japanese in 1941, Ms. Cooper has crafted an intricate web of emotionally charged stories of courage, hope, and enduring friendship that will lift your spirits even as they expose the realities of wartime occupation and the almost impossible choices faced by individuals in mixed-race, international families at the beginning of World War II."

—JACK MAISANO, former president of the American Chamber of Commerce in Hong Kong and the China Institute in New York, and publisher of *The Asian Wall Street Journal Weekly* and *Asiaweek* magazine.

"*Dragonfly Dreams* presented a fictionalized and shorter time period of Nini Liu's life, a younger American in China. This can be viewed as a case study of war, of complex relationships between people and countries, people from different nationalities. I want to imagine the conversations between teachers and students, or parents and children, in book groups, about the history of wars, diseases, hunger, and so much more. This is a very timely study guide for all. As the story ends, I am hopeful that the dragonfly lands on some of us, changing us for the better."

—LULU LIM COPELAND, executive director, Tennessee-China Network

"I read this book in one sitting on a rainy day. That's always a good sign for a book. While the story is set within a specific moment of historical turmoil, it is a universal story about family, friendship, hardship, survival—and most importantly to me, it is a testament to the bright, hopeful resilience and strength of youth. Go, you young people, GO!

—DOUGLAS MCCALLIE, five-time Emmy nominated executive producer and showrunner of *Survivor*

"Nini is a Chinese-American girl who narrates the story of her times during the Japanese occupation of China. She is sequestered with her American mother and Chinese father, siblings, and family friends, and tells us the big story of war's horrors through many small events. It is a story of resilience and keeping hope alive. I will get copies for my grandchildren. They should know this history. We adults should also read this book. It will help us not to repeat our past mistakes."

—MILENKO MATANOVIC, author of *Meandering Rivers and Square Tomatoes, The Case for Everyday Democracy*

"*Dragonfly Dreams* is a riveting tale from start to finish. The steady suspense ensuing from continual twists and turns easily entices a one-session read."

—MARGARET SCHUETTE, editor of *Journey Between Two Worlds*, a memoir by Karola M. Schuette

"*Dragonfly Dreams* is a masterfully-written story of WWII like never before, giving a child's intimate look at the injustice and brutality of the Japanese occupation of China and its effects on her Chinese-American family. Readers will share Nini's raw emotions, wanting to kick and scream at the Japanese soldiers just as she does."

—DANIELLE KOEHLER, author of *The Other Forest*

"I can't wait for my students to read *Dragonfly Dreams*. It opened my eyes to a new perspective on World War II as I instantly connected with Nini and her family."

—CINDY GASTON, teacher and instructional coach, Hamilton County Schools, Tennessee

"*Dragonfly Dreams* is an outstanding YA novel set in mid-twentieth-century China and based upon the author's family history there. Nini is a delight. She's brave, loyal, loving, and despite all her hardships, she believes a better future is coming for herself and her family. The dragonfly means change is coming and it also means good luck. Can it be both? Recommended.

—LYNDA DURRANT, author of *My Last Skirt: The Story of Mary Campbell* and *The Beaded Moccasins*

Dragonfly Dreams

by Eleanor McCallie Cooper

ISBN 978-1-64663-421-7

Map created by Evie Zhu
Cover Design by Kellie Emery

Published by

 köehlerbooks™

3705 Shore Drive
Virginia Beach, VA 23455
800-435-4811
www.koehlerbooks.com

DRAGONFLY DREAMS

BASED ON A TRUE STORY

ELEANOR McCALLIE COOPER

VIRGINIA BEACH
CAPE CHARLES

Dedicated to Grace McCallie Divine Liu

Four years is a long time and if I tried to tell only a part of what we've been through since I last wrote I would fill a book.

November 20, 1945

TABLE OF CONTENTS

FOREWORD

BY KATHERINE PATERSON

*S*ince my own parents were in China from 1923 to 1940, and I was born there in 1932, this family's story reminded me in many ways of my own. Even more parallels existed between their daughter Julia (Ju-lan in Chinese, nicknamed Nini) and me. We were born the same year. We both began our primary education in English-speaking schools and lived for a time in port cities divided into concessions independently governed by various Western authorities— the Lius in Tianjin, the Womeldorfs (my family) in Shanghai. And if the previous sentence makes no sense, please read this book.

Japan invaded China in 1937. I can well remember how life changed when we moved out of the protected French Concession of Shanghai into Japanese-occupied territory. But US citizens were ordered out of China by the American embassy in late 1940. Grace Liu (Nini's mother) did not follow that order. She chose to remain with her Chinese husband and half-Chinese children. After Pearl Harbor, the protected foreign concessions disappeared, and Grace was declared an "enemy alien."

In *Dragonfly Dreams,* the author's imagination goes to work on those same events. How would Grace's ten-year-old daughter have felt and acted during this perilous time? As a child in China, I know how I felt, certainly at times as fearful as Nini, never quite as recklessly brave, though I'd have admired her kicking that cruel soldier and wished I had the nerve.

This is an account of family love and sacrifice, interwoven with the story of Nini's treasured, war-threatened friendship.

The author tells us her book is based on a true story, the historical dates and facts forming a structure. "But," she says, "the content of the story, the letter that goes inside the envelope, is fictional." As a wise person has said, "The truth of the imagination is not imaginary truth."

Katherine Paterson, two-time Newberry Award winner for Bridge to Terabithia *and* Jacob Have I Loved, *author of thirty books for young readers, National Book Award, and Hans Christian Andersen Award for lifetime contribution to children's literature.*

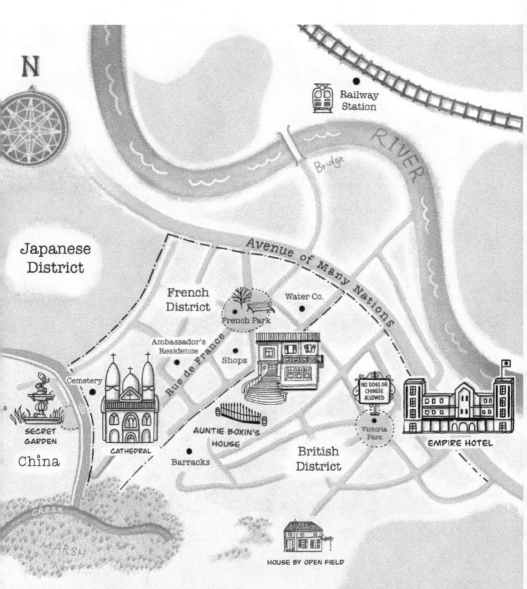

Map of Dragonfly Dreams

CREATED BY EVIE ZHU

*S*unlight sparkled in the grass and flashed off the pool of water. At first, I didn't see what landed on my arm—the shivering wings of silver, blue, and green, the long narrow body, and the big round head with the bulging black eyes that seemed to see in every direction.

I started to reach for it, but Chiyoko stopped me.

"No, don't hurt it."

"Why not?" I asked.

"It's a dragonfly. When a dragonfly lands on you, it's good luck. It's a sign that change is coming. You better watch your dreams, Nini."

It flew off, wings fluttering rapidly, and then changed directions and hovered over us. I lifted my hand hoping it would land again, but it flew quickly out of reach. Two others appeared—then suddenly there were five or six, and more, flitting around Chiyoko's head, their blue-green wings reflecting an iridescent glow. We began to flutter too, trying neither to catch them nor to chase them away—dancing with them in the sunlight, holding our arms out like wings, hovering, rising, falling, laughing.

Part One

CHAPTER 1

December 5, 1941
A coastal city in China

*I*t was the day before my tenth birthday. Chiyoko and I were walking home from school.

When we usually reached the Avenue of Many Nations, we parted to go home in different directions, but this day we stopped dead in our tracks. Japanese soldiers were blocking the way, barking orders, and shoving people to the side of the street.

A soldier wearing a dark helmet had a rifle with a sword at the end, pointing directly at us.

Chiyoko froze, but I saw an opening in the crowd, and dodging the soldier, I pulled her away, stepping quickly to a place in the crowd where we could see down the street.

A shiny black car was moving slowly toward us. Rows of Japanese soldiers marched stiffly behind it. I could feel as well as hear the *thump, thump, thump* of their heavy boots against the pavement.

Suddenly a rickshaw swerved into the street. The Chinese puller didn't seem to notice the black car or the soldiers as he shouted in English, "Out of way! I have French ambassador's wife!"

The passenger was a woman in a fur coat, wearing a black hat with dark netting covering her face. She held her arm around a boy with blonde hair dressed in a heavy coat.

Usually a rickshaw carrying a foreigner, especially someone important like the French ambassador's wife, could get through any crowd easily. The puller ignored a Japanese officer's command to stop, continuing down the street as if he didn't hear him. Then the officer moved toward him, lifted the butt of his rifle in the air, and struck the rickshaw puller hard on the head.

The puller groaned and crumpled to the ground, still holding on to the poles as he fell. The French ambassador's wife and the boy were thrown forward. A man next to me tried to help her but was shoved back by two soldiers. The man yelled, "Call the police!" But no one came.

The woman in the rickshaw straightened her hat, then grabbed the boy's hand and climbed out, stepping right on top of the fallen rickshaw man.

The Japanese officer yelled again, and two soldiers quickly dragged the rickshaw and the limp man out of the way of the oncoming car.

Chiyoko, pushing next to me, stiffened as if she saw or heard something I didn't. "Oh no," she said. "My father. He warned me—"

The soldiers stood at attention as the car passed by. The crowd stayed quiet, but as soon as the car passed, everyone began pushing against each other, trying to move in all directions.

"We better get out of here, Nini." Chiyoko grabbed my arm. "Come on! You can't go that way." She gestured in the direction I usually went home. "Not with these soldiers here. I know another way."

Not having a chance to question her, I chased Chiyoko across the street. She broke into a run, and when she turned into an alley, I almost lost her. The alley was a narrow passage behind the buildings, stacked with all sorts of junk. Chiyoko seemed to glide through like a fish in water, but I tripped on some broken tiles, bumped my head on a pipe sticking out of the wall, and nearly choked on a clothesline stretched across the alley. My heart pounding, I dodged ladders and bamboo poles, bicycle parts and broken carts, and nearly gagged on sour smells from earthenware pots.

I finally caught up with Chiyoko as she slowed at a wooden gate and pushed it open. I followed her through. She shut the gate behind us, sighing with relief.

We were in someone's garden, but it looked abandoned. There was a fountain in the middle of the garden covered in vines. The statue on top of the fountain was a fish that looked like it was trying to swim out of the vines. The house was dark and shuttered, surrounded by a crumbling brick wall with glass shards on top.

Chiyoko leaned against the wall next to the gate. I fell against my knapsack beside her.

"You don't need to run so fast," I panted. "No one is following us."

"I know," she said. "But I couldn't stop."

She took off her knapsack, dropped it to the ground, and then squatted beside it. I slumped down beside her.

Chiyoko and I looked alike in so many ways, but we were different in so many others. We were about the same height and both wore our hair in long braids. When we were dressed in the school uniform—a navy-blue skirt and a white blouse with a sailor collar and navy-blue tie—the other girls couldn't tell us apart and just called us "the little Chinese girls." That angered Chiyoko, but she didn't say anything. She couldn't brag that her father was Japanese, not then, anyway, when the Japanese were causing so much trouble. But she was proud that her hair was blacker and straighter than mine and her skin was fairer. She had a narrower face and was slimmer than me. I had a rather round face and body. My eyes were hazel, and I had more of a bridge on my nose, which made me look more like the foreign girls.

We attended an international school where most of the girls were from foreign families living in China. I had a hard time telling the French girls from the British or the Russians from the Poles; they all looked *foreign* to me. What made me mad was that they treated me as if *I* were the foreigner in China!

I felt I could stand up to them because I was American. Da, who is Chinese, married Ma when he was studying engineering in New York, and that's where I was born. I guess you could say I'm half-American and half-Chinese, but all they saw was my Chinese side. Like the time Chiyoko and I were walking together when two British girls, I think they were sisters, were coming from the opposite direction, and the older one said, "You Chinese girls better get out of the way when we pass." Chiyoko looked down and moved aside. I just stood there and yelled, "I belong here more than—" Before I could get the words out, Chiyoko pulled my arm and jerked me back, causing me to trip over my own feet. The girls just walked on, giggling and poking each other.

Leaning against the wall, I finally caught my breath.

"What's happening, Chiyoko?"

"My father told me something might happen today," she said. "When I saw the car and the soldiers, I wondered if this is what he meant."

She paused a moment, then she turned and looked straight at me.

"He told me to tell you . . . to tell your mother. Nini, you must tell your mother to be careful!"

"Why? Why my mother?"

"Because she's American. My father said to tell your mother to stay inside for a while. Not to go outside."

"What does that have to do with the soldiers?"

"I think it has to do with the car."

"Did you see who was in it?"

"No, I couldn't see. Too many people in the way."

"But I don't understand what that has to do with my mother anyway."

"I don't know exactly, but my father thinks she might be in danger."

Chiyoko jumped up, looking around. "We need to find a place

to leave messages." She began moving her hands over the wall as if she were a blind person looking for a doorknob.

"What are you doing?"

"I used to come here. My parents knew the family who lived here before they left last year."

Many people left last year . . . they locked their houses and just left. Most of them were foreigners who lived in the foreign districts. You see, although we were in China, we didn't live *in* China. Where we lived was divided into sections, and each section was owned by a different country and had their own laws. England owned a district. France had a district. So did Russia and Italy and other European countries. Japan claimed a large section, built like a fortress.

"My father was their doctor, and when he made a house call, I used to play with their daughter."

Chiyoko's father, Dr. Mori, was a very kind and well-known doctor. He had a medical clinic in the Chinese part of the city where he served whoever came. Chiyoko told me he had come to China to work at the Japanese hospital, and that's where he met Chiyoko's mother who was a nurse. Because she was Chinese and marriage with Chinese was forbidden for the Japanese, he was forced to leave the hospital. That's why they started their own clinic and lived in the apartment above it.

"When I played with their daughter," she said, continuing to move her hands along the bricks, "we used to leave secret messages in a hiding place."

Her hand hit a brick that was sticking out a little from the others. "Look, Nini!"

She wiggled the brick and pulled on it until it came out from the wall.

"You see," said Chiyoko triumphantly. "It's only half a brick, and there's a space for us to leave messages."

"But why will we need to do that?" I asked, growing agitated with Chiyoko. "I'll see you at school on Monday, just like always."

She paused. "Just in case . . . if you ever want to tell me something or if you hear something. You can leave me a message and tell me to meet you here. I'll check and see if there is a message, and then I'll meet you."

Chiyoko put the brick back in the wall.

"Now, fold and flatten your message, stick it inside the hole and put the brick back. I'll find it."

She started looking around again. "Let's leave something at this spot so we know where the secret hiding place is."

The wall was crumbling in many places, and Chiyoko began looking for loose bricks on the ground. I began picking up bricks, too.

When we had a small pile, Chiyoko said, "I better go. My mother will be worried."

Her mother ran the clinic, but she also worried about Chiyoko all the time.

Chiyoko began fumbling in her knapsack.

"Nini, I don't know if I will see you on your birthday." She pulled out a small red box. "Here," she said and pushed the box into my hand.

The top of the box fell off when Chiyoko moved her hand away. Staring up at me were the bulging black eyes of a dragonfly with shining wings of silver blue.

Memories flooded my mind. We had been playing one day when a dragonfly landed on my arm. I was afraid of it at first and wanted to chase it away, but Chiyoko told me not to.

"If a dragonfly lands on you, it's good luck," she said. "You'll have a dream—a dragonfly dream. It means change is coming."

I remembered how we danced that day fluttering our arms as other dragonflies flew around us, laughing in the afternoon light. I smiled, and so did Chiyoko.

I pulled out the dragonfly, and the necklace chain fell across my hand. Before I could thank her, Chiyoko startled me by saying in a serious tone, "I'll miss you, Nini."

"Why do you say that? I'll see you at school Monday."

"I hope so," she said.

Chiyoko put her arms through the straps of the knapsack. "You can go home that way." She pointed with her forehead toward the other side of the garden. I looked in the direction she indicated, but all I saw were some bushes. "There's a hole in the wall over there. It goes to the French district."

"How will you get home?"

"I'll go back to the alley and turn on the next street. It's not far. My parent's clinic is around the corner from here."

I had never been to the clinic, even with Chiyoko, because it was in the Chinese part of the city, and Ma said it was too dangerous for me to go there. I didn't realize that we had run so far—all the way through the alley to China.

"I better go." Chiyoko paused at the gate. Her jet-black hair had come loose during the run and some wisps of hair fell across her face, which seemed paler than usual; her usually bright eyes were moist. In that moment she seemed much older. She went out the gate and closed it behind her.

Immediately, as soon as the gate closed, I felt alone and anxious to get home. Ma would be worried about me too. I put the lid on the dragonfly box, stuffed it in my knapsack, and headed for the other side of the garden.

Behind the bushes, I found exactly what Chiyoko had said—a place in the wall where the bricks had fallen out. I took my knapsack off and shimmied sideways through the narrow gap, pulling my knapsack after me.

CHAPTER 2

*O*n the other side of the wall, I pushed past some oleander bushes only to discover I was in a cemetery with large flat gravestones. I didn't know where I was or who was buried here, but I followed a path between the stones to the back of a building. When the path came to an end, I realized I was behind a cathedral.

The Cathedral of St. Georges was the tallest building in the French district. Everything on the cathedral was done in threes—three crosses, three domes, and three arches. Everyone knew the cathedral, and I had come this way with Amah and knew my way home from there.

The Rue de France was as busy as usual for a Friday afternoon. A French policeman stood on a platform in the middle of the intersection in his khaki uniform, blowing his whistle, stopping traffic in one direction with his white-gloved hand held straight out. With his other white-gloved hand flicking rapidly, he directed the traffic to go one way or the other, bicycles and bicycle carts, pedicabs and mini-trucks. But this didn't stop the drivers from yelling and honking at each other to get out of the way.

When he blew his shrill whistle and held out his hand to halt traffic, I ran across quickly and barely dodged a man on a bicycle cart.

"Hey, watch where you're going, you scamp!" he yelled and swerved, almost losing his load of baskets as he barely missed a farmer's vegetable cart.

I ran past the government buildings with their tall wrought iron gates behind which was the French ambassador's residence. I ran past the shops with white and green awnings—the butcher shop, the café, and the bakery where our cook, Sun, came for rolls in the mornings.

A small group of children played in the French park while their Chinese nannies chattered on the benches along a row of fruit trees. I was too much in a hurry to look and see if Amah, our nursemaid, was there with my five-year-old sister, Mei-mei, or my baby brother, Weilin.

Chiyoko thought it funny that I lived in the French district when neither of my parents were French. But lots of people lived in the French district who weren't French, and, besides, we lived there because my father was the chief engineer of the water company, which was also in the French district.

The water company was not far from the French park, in a compound surrounded by a wall with a gate. The guard on duty that day knew me well and opened the gate wide when he saw me coming. I didn't even say hello as I ran past him.

The guard called after me, "What's the matter, Little Missy?"

Bounding up the stairs to our apartment, I burst through the door, eager to tell Ma what had happened. I didn't think someone else might be there, but I ran smack into a pair of hairy arms that wrapped around my neck and held me so tight I could hardly breathe.

"Hey, what's the big hurry, Baboon?" asked a husky voice with an Irish accent.

I knew at once it was Tooner. I usually loved it when Tooner came. He never knocked and would announce himself with a boisterous, "The tuner's here!" when he came to tune Ma's piano. Everyone just called him Tooner. He was a chesty, red-bearded Irishman who had lived in China forever. He was always full of jokes and funny songs, but I didn't feel like joking around.

"Let me go!" I squirmed and pushed away.

"Nini, don't be rude. Say hello to Tooner," my mother said, sitting at the piano on the other side of the living room.

"Hello, Tooner. Excuse me," I said, straightening my braids. Then I turned quickly to Ma. "But, Ma, the Japanese—"

Tooner interrupted. "Ah, my little Baboon, don't worry 'bout them Japs."

Calling me *Baboon* was Tooner's way of teasing me about being part Chinese, as if I were part monkey or wild animal.

"The Japs are like mosquitoes—irritating for the moment, but just keep swatting at 'em and they'll soon go away," Tooner said, picking up his tuning fork and putting it in his big leather bag.

"The Brits've been here a hundred years and they'll jolly well be here another hundred." He closed his tool bag. "Why, I was born here. It's my home as much as the Chinese. It's the Japs that don't belong."

"But Tooner, this was different today. They hit a rickshaw man. I think they killed him!"

Tooner picked up his bag as if it had feathers in it, not tools. "The coolie was probably in the way."

"But he was pulling the French ambassador's wife!"

"But were they inside the French district?"

"No, just outside. On the Avenue of Many Nations."

The Avenue of Many Nations was the main road from the train station to the foreign districts.

"The black car was no doubt headed to the Japanese district, and the soldiers were making sure it got there safely. Well, don't fret your little head over it," Tooner said moving toward the door. "They won't bother us here. These districts are foreign countries to them. It'd be like declaring war on Europe. And believe me, the Japs don't want the French or the Brits on their backs right now."

Tooner reached for my head and gave me a "buzz." He laughed at me squirming to get out from under his grip as he rubbed the top of my head with his knuckles. When he let go, he turned back toward the room, as if he had forgotten something. He put his bag down on the table, reached into the side pocket and pulled out a card.

"Here," Tooner said, handing me a picture of an old man. "This is St. Patrick. He'll protect ya . . . see here."

The old man in the picture was wearing a long white robe and standing next to a rock. One hand held a long cane that curved at the top, and his other hand pointed to snakes that seemed to be racing as fast as they could to the sea.

"Ya see, there, if St. Patrick can chase the snakes from Ireland, he can chase the Japs from China, too, quick as a wink."

With that, he winked at me. His blue eyes twinkled, and it seemed to me that the freckles on his face winked too.

"Remember what I taught you," Tooner said, as he slung the tool bag over his shoulder. "The best way to get their goat is to whistle. Just keep whistling, my little Baboon."

Tooner headed out the door and down the stairs, whistling a tune that made me want to follow. Resisting the urge, I turned back into the apartment.

Despite Ma correcting my manners earlier, she didn't get up or even say goodbye to Tooner. She was playing a Chopin piece she often played when she wanted to be left alone. I could tell she hadn't been out that day because she was wearing a casual dress and slippers. Her soft brown hair was loosely tucked behind her ears rather than pulled into a bun like she did when she went out. She seldom needed to go out anyway. Sun went to the market, and Amah did the other chores when she took Mei-mei or Weilin out. Ma probably knew nothing about the soldiers.

I dropped my knapsack on the sofa and slipped St. Patrick's picture in the side pocket. I started to reach for Chiyoko's gift, but before I could I heard loud footsteps coming up the stairs.

It was too early for Da to come home, but there he stood at the door, out of breath and red in the face. Da could run up those stairs on a normal day without skipping a beat. Something must have caused him to be winded and red in the face.

Ma stopped playing the piano and immediately went over to greet him. She smiled as she took his coat and looked happy to see him. Da was tall for a Chinese man and had a good build. He had a round face, thick black hair, and clear dark eyes.

"Da!" I blurted out.

I was eager to tell him what I had seen—how Japanese soldiers had blocked the road, how they stopped the French ambassador's wife, and maybe even killed the rickshaw driver.

But all I could say was, "I'm so glad you're home."

Da didn't seem to hear me. "Sit down, both of you. I have something to tell you."

Ma called to Sun to make some tea. Then she motioned me to sit on the sofa with her.

Our apartment was Western style with just a few Chinese things. In front of the sofa was a blue and white Mongolian rug and a low round table. The table was made of rosewood with carvings of fruits and flowers and birds. Mei-mei and I often played at the rosewood table with the brass monkey. Da told us the monkey had magic powers and his staff could be a sword or a needle, so one time Mei-mei poured ink on it to see if it would become a pen. The ink left a dark stain on the table. I sat on the sofa near the dark stain.

Da paced on the Mongolian rug while we got settled. "I'm being forced to take sides," he said. "Either I cooperate with the Japanese or . . ."

"Cooperate how?" Ma asked.

"I have to do what they say, or I'm fired."

"But you're the chief engineer. They can't fire you!" Ma exclaimed.

"Don't let them, Da," I blurted out, as determined as Ma.

"Unfortunately, they have the upper hand now."

"I never thought it would come to this," Ma said. "You are the first Chinese to run the water company. There is no one with your education to take your place. How did they get the upper hand?"

"I should have seen it coming when Mr. Yasemoto started working at the company," he said.

"Didn't Mr. Yasemoto come to help you?" Ma asked.

"Ah! Mr. Yasemoto was only pretending to help. The Japanese placed him at the water company to learn from me. Today he came with soldiers and told me they were taking over. I was given a choice. Either I cooperate or—"

He walked over to the desk where he kept his cigarettes.

"They can't take over if you don't let them!" I wanted my father to say no! I wanted all the Chinese to say no!

"Why would anyone cooperate with them?" Ma pounded her fist against the arm of the sofa.

"Some people want to keep their jobs and salaries, so they do what the Japanese tell them and hope it will be over soon. And besides—" He paused and lit a cigarette. "The ones who stay take the jobs of those who refuse." His face got redder.

Sun brought in a small tray with three cups of tea. He set them on the rosewood table and left. No one picked up the teacups.

When Ma spoke, her voice was softer. "When we first met in New York, you told me you wanted to help China build a modern water system, to be a modern nation. Is that dream lost now?"

"I've done all I can. I don't know what will happen if the company falls into Japanese hands," my father said in despair.

"When the American Embassy warned me last year to leave, I didn't think the Japanese could take over . . . how could a small island take over a huge country like China?" Ma said.

"Do you wish you had left when the others did?" Da asked her. Many of Ma's friends had left last year.

"Not at all!" Ma insisted. "As long as you stay, I will stay. I still don't believe they will harm us, not as long as you're head of the water company."

"But that's just it," he said, then smashed out his cigarette in the ashtray on his desk.

"What do you mean?" Ma asked.

"Mr. Yasemoto told me today—" He turned and faced Ma. "He told me it doesn't look good for the chief engineer to have an American wife. He's forcing me to choose between my family and the company."

"But . . . you can't quit!"

"You know I would never leave you!" Da walked across the room and stood by the piano. He was shaking.

I got up and walked over to comfort him. "But, Da, Tooner says we're safe here. The French district is like a foreign country."

"Well, Tooner has his head in the clouds. He can't see what's coming. He's like all the other foreigners. He can't see what's right in front of him."

Da turned and looked out the window as he spoke. "Today, more Japanese troops were pouring into the train station, and I heard an important general arrived to take command."

The black car! Suddenly, I realized why the Japanese soldiers blocked the road, why they were marching behind the black car. The man in the car was the general who had come to take command!

I wasn't concerned at that moment about the Japanese soldiers, or the general for that matter. I was thinking about Chiyoko. She seemed to know something, something her father had told her.

"I have to go," I said and turned for the door. My father grabbed my arm and pulled me back. I squirmed in his grasp.

"I want to see Chiyoko!"

I had barely gotten her name out when my father looked hard at me and said, "I don't think you'll be seeing Chiyoko anymore, Nini."

"What do you mean?" I cried.

"I heard today the Japanese are sending wives and children back to Japan."

What? Is Chiyoko leaving? I couldn't believe what Da was saying. I didn't blame him for not cooperating, but surely he was wrong about Chiyoko.

"But her mother is Chinese!" I thought that gave her permission to stay.

"Yes, I know. But they're in a difficult situation now. Because her father is Japanese, they may send his family to Japan. Chiyoko and her mother will have to stay low for a while."

Then I remembered the warning Chiyoko's father had sent Ma.

CHAPTER 3

*S*unday night I had a terrible dream. Bees were swarming into
my room, buzzing around my head. The bees kept coming in
long straight lines, the buzzing getting louder. In my dream, I
went to shut the window, but it was already shut. The bees were flying
through the glass! I couldn't stop them from coming in, and I couldn't
stop the noise.

It took me a while to realize I was actually hearing something—a
sound I didn't recognize at first. It grew louder and closer. It was a
grating sound, a low groaning noise. As I opened my eyes, I heard
another sound—*thump, thump, thump* in a steady deafening rhythm.
I recognized that sound!

I threw back my blankets and ran to the window. Pressing my
face against the cold glass, nothing looked familiar. It was early
morning, and no one was going about their daily business. Only a
line of slowly moving trucks, dark and heavy, groaning in low gear.
Behind the trucks marched Japanese soldiers, row after row, in olive
drab uniforms with heavy boots flapping against the pavement in a
throbbing rhythm—*thump, thump, thump.*

A knot gripped my stomach as I gasped to catch my breath. I
knew I would not see Chiyoko that day.

With the rhythm of the soldiers' boots throbbing in my ears, I hurried to wake my parents, but they were already up and still dressed in their night clothes. Da was hunched over the big wooden radio in the living room. Ma was leaning over Da's shoulder.

"Wait! I heard something," Ma said anxiously.

Da was changing the channels with his ear close to the speaker.

"It's only static," Da said, continuing to turn the dial.

"I thought I heard English." Ma reached for the dial. She depended on the radio for news in English, but that day, only buzzing came from the wooden box.

"I can't get anything," Da said. "Even the Chinese station is static."

My mind felt static too, all fuzzy and confused like the radio sounds. Everyone had said we were safe here, that Japan would never enter the foreign districts. So what had changed? Why had the Japanese soldiers crossed that invisible barrier, like bees going through glass?

Just then we heard a knock on the door.

"Go to the back room," Da commanded. Ma and I stepped toward the hall, but when I heard the voice at the door, I turned quickly back into the living room.

Da opened the door, and Paul Thompson stood there. He was a friend to our family, the American director of the YMCA and married to a Chinese woman. I knew their son Tommy Thompson, a half-and-half like me, but he thought he was better because he had an American last name. Although we weren't close friends, I was hoping Tommy had come with his father.

"Paul, come in!" Da was smiling, obviously relieved, as he held the door open.

Mr. Thompson was the tallest man I'd ever known. When he ducked his head to enter and removed his hat, it looked like he was bowing to Da. I was sorry Tommy wasn't with him.

"It's so good to see you, Paul." Ma came back into the living room. "What a welcome sight you are. Won't you sit down?"

"I can't stay," he said.

I had to crane my neck to look up at Mr. Thompson.

"Hello, Nini," he said.

I was about to ask, "Where's Tommy?" but the words stuck in my throat, and I stared at him. Ma didn't seem concerned about my manners that morning.

"I'm making the rounds, telling as many people as I can," Mr. Thompson said. "The Japanese have jammed all the airwaves."

"That must be why I can't get any news on the radio," Da said, shutting the door behind Mr. Thompson.

"Yes, that's why, but I was able to get through on my short-wave radio."

"What have you heard?" Ma asked, pushing past me.

"Japan attacked the United States at Pearl Harbor this morning. The US has declared war on Japan."

"I can't believe it!" Ma's hand covered her mouth. She stepped back and her hair fell loose.

"They attacked early Sunday morning," Mr. Thompson said. "They caught the US completely by surprise. Destroyed the fleet. I wanted you to know right away."

"What's Pearl Harbor?" I tugged on Ma, but she ignored me, her eyes and ears fixed on Mr. Thompson.

Mr. Thompson turned to me. "It's the American naval base in Hawaii, Nini."

But that didn't help me much. Hawaii was far away, and I didn't see how it explained the Japanese soldiers marching in front of our house.

"But Sunday was yesterday," I said, still confused.

"No, Nini, it wasn't yesterday. The Japanese bombed Pearl Harbor this morning. It's Monday in China when it's Sunday in Hawaii."

"It doesn't make sense," said Ma, staring straight ahead, as if talking to someone else. "Why would Japan attack Pearl Harbor?" Then she looked back at Mr. Thompson. "Do they want to take over America too?"

Da had been quiet, but now he spoke forcefully. "They aren't interested in America! Don't you see?"

"I don't understand," Ma said. I figured if she had been puzzled over how a small country could take over a big country, she must have been doubly puzzled how it could take over two large ones.

"They aren't trying to take over America. Don't you see! They only want to prevent the American fleet from letting them take over here!" Da's face was turning red. "Only the US forces in the Pacific could prevent Japan from taking over China."

"You're right. Britain and France are at war in Europe," Mr. Thompson said. "Only the American Navy could stop them. That's why the Japanese marched into the foreign districts this morning. They no longer fear being stopped."

"Now I know why Mr. Yasemoto said it didn't look good for the chief engineer to have an American wife. He knew Japan would be at war with America." Da turned to Mr. Thompson. "Has there been any resistance here?"

"No. I think the Japanese took over not only the French district but all the foreign territories this morning, without resistance."

"Well, they know China can't stop them. The Japanese already control the rest of the city. The Chinese army is no better than a fly swatter!" Da always smoked when he was angry, and he started fumbling around on his desk looking for his cigarettes.

"I'd better be going. I have to tell as many families as I can," Mr. Thompson said, turning toward the door.

"Thanks for coming, Paul, and please be careful," Ma said as she followed him to the door.

Paul Thompson lowered his head to exit and put his hat back on. Ma watched him go down the stairs. As soon as he was gone, Da charged, "Where are my cigarettes?"

Just then I caught sight of a pack of cigarettes under the brass monkey's raised leg. He was dressed like a warrior and had one leg up as if he was going to attack. Mei-mei had been playing at the rosewood table with the brass monkey and must have put Da's cigarettes there.

I quickly handed him the pack of cigarettes. Ma kept talking without paying attention to me.

"I wish I could talk to my mother. I hope everyone at home is all right!"

"You don't need to worry about your family. They live thousands of miles from Pearl Harbor. I'm sure they're all right," Da said, letting out a long puff of smoke.

"But the American news must be full of Pearl Harbor right now. No one will be paying attention to what's happening in China," Ma said, looking hopelessly at Da.

"Your family doesn't have any idea that you are under Japanese occupation now." Da threw the pack of cigarettes on the desk. "It's disgusting! Japan has taken over China without even being noticed."

Ma walked over to the window and looked out at the overcast sky.

"Do you really think no one even knows what has happened to us? I must write to them."

No matter what happened, Ma always wrote a letter home. She sent one every week to her mother in Tennessee and almost as often to her brother. The letters from her family arrived on Tuesday when the mail boat pulled into the harbor, and the very next day, she'd have a letter on the return boat.

Suddenly the distressed look on Ma's face changed, and she turned away from the window, addressing us excitedly.

"This may be the best news we could hear!"

"Ma! How can you say that?"

"I know my country, Nini. If America is attacked, she will fight back. It is only a matter of time before US troops will rescue us. I know they will come!"

She turned back to the window and was looking up at the sky, as if she expected to see American planes flying over at that very moment.

"Move away from the window!" Da yelled. "We don't know what we are facing now. Japan is at war with America. You may be in danger."

Ma lingered at the window a little longer, then pulled the curtains.

"We have to be careful of everything we do or say. The last thing you should do now is write a letter home. You could be accused of being a spy."

"How could I be a spy? My letters are only to my family," Ma challenged.

Da picked up newspapers from the desk and crumpled them in his hands. Tossing them in the fireplace, he lit a match. Da added more paper until he had a lively flame.

"Bring that to me, Nini," Da instructed, pointing to a letter on the rosewood table.

"But that's Nana's letter," I stammered.

Grandmother Julia had lived with us when I was born in New York. I was named after her. My name is Julia in English, and Ju-Lian in Chinese, which means Red Lotus. But I called her Nana, and she called me Nini.

It was a fat letter because Nana had enclosed pictures and newspaper clippings. She always wrote a special message just for me and included news about my cousin. I had not seen my cousin since I left for China. Without Nana's letters, I wouldn't know anything about my cousin or Ma's family.

"You heard me."

Da's face was illuminated by the flames, but I saw no warmth there as he added, "And get those in the dresser."

He twisted another sheet of newspaper, and the flame shot up.

I looked at Ma, hoping she would stop him. Ma came over to the table, picked up the letter, and pulled out the pictures.

"All of it," he said. "The least little thing could be used against you. Letters. Pictures. Newspaper clippings. Anything that shows you have connections in America and that you send news back and forth. You never know what will happen. Get the others."

I stared in disbelief as Ma handed him the letter and pictures, then turned away. She headed for the bedroom and didn't watch as the letter caught fire and the photographs crackled in the flames.

I followed my mother and watched her open the top drawer of the dresser and pull out a bundle of letters.

"Ma! Don't give him Nana's letters!"

Ma sighed and sat on the edge of the bed, holding the letters tightly in her lap. "Oh, Nini, I know these letters mean everything to you and to me, too. They are our only tie to home."

"Why is he burning them? You're not a spy."

"No, I'm not. But he wants to protect us."

"But why, Ma?"

"I can't explain it now, Nini." Ma looked only briefly at the letters, then handed them to me. "Here, take these to your father." I could tell by the tears in her eyes that this was not the time to talk.

CHAPTER 4

Christmas passed, and still the American planes hadn't come. The mail stopped, and no more letters made it across the Pacific Ocean to our port city in northern China. It was the first Christmas I hadn't received presents from Ma's family—the usual gifts of pajamas and socks, a party dress, a doll, and puzzles. The usual Christmas Eve dinner with roast pork and the Christmas day party with eggnog and Sun's cake didn't happen either. Sun had been a pastry chef's apprentice at the Empire Hotel and every Christmas he made us a seven-layer cake with smooth, sweet chocolate icing.

But what I missed most was going to school. It wasn't school so much that I missed, but seeing Chiyoko.

I hadn't seen Chiyoko for three weeks. I had a dream that she had gone to the garden and was looking everywhere for a message from me. I woke worrying about her and wondering if she had left a message for me. Now I understood why she had insisted on the secret hiding place!

Early that morning, I heard Da on a phone call.

"That will do no good!" he yelled into the phone. He hung up and told Ma he had to go to the office—the workers were holding a meeting. He left in a hurry.

Ma was busy packing. Amah was tending to Mei-mei and Weilin in the back room since she couldn't take them to the park anymore. Sun was cleaning up after breakfast. No one was paying attention to me, so I thought no one would notice. I could get to the secret garden and back before anyone knew I was gone. I grabbed my knapsack and left the apartment without telling anyone where I was going.

The morning air was bitter cold. I wished I had worn a heavy coat instead of my jacket, but I didn't dare go back, and besides, I thought, my journey would be quick.

Since the Japanese had taken over, few people were outdoors, and business seemed to have come to a halt.

I had heard Da and Sun talking a few days earlier about where the Japanese guards were posted, so I knew which streets to avoid. I didn't want to take the sidewalks along the wide streets, so I decided to go through the park. In the French Park, the mingling of languages no longer floated from the sandbox like it did when the amahs used to come with foreign children. The trees were bare and the benches empty. I crossed the park without seeing anyone.

Not many people were at the shops with the green and white-striped awnings. No sweet smell of warm bread or aroma of coffee greeted me. The café had only a few customers, and the bakery was closed. I avoided the sidewalk in front of the French ambassador's residence by taking a path behind bushes that a child could easily hide behind. When I neared the intersection at the Rue de France, I wondered how I would cross unnoticed.

I pressed close to a building until I could peek around the corner to see if Japanese guards were where the French policeman used to direct traffic with his shrill whistle and white-gloved hands. I could see the mist of my own breath in the late December air. I watched my breath for a moment before peeking around the corner.

Standing on the police box were four Japanese soldiers looking in all directions and carrying rifles with bayonets attached to them.

I jerked back and held my breath. I pulled my jacket tight around me as if that made me smaller and invisible. My heart pounded as I realized no one knew where I was. *If I get caught by the soldiers, who will know? Will my parents find me?* I shivered.

A few deliverymen with wagons loaded with goods and a few servants doing duties for their households were the only people out that day. Just then an old sweet-potato man came by pushing his cart. It had a small furnace where he baked the potatoes and kept them warm. He used to walk down the residential streets and beep a horn to let children know he was approaching. That was my favorite sound on cold days, as hot sweet potatoes made a great snack. But today his furnace was cold, and he wasn't selling anything.

The Japanese soldier blew a whistle. The sweet potato man stopped so abruptly that potatoes rolled off the back of the cart. He didn't seem to notice, or maybe he was afraid to lean down to pick them up. So he just kept walking across the intersection when the guards gave him the command to proceed.

I picked up the potatoes nearest me and ran to give them to the man. By the time I reached him, he was almost across the street. He took the potatoes and said in a whisper, "Thank you, Little Missy."

I continued walking alongside the sweet potato man until we reached the Cathedral of St. Georges with its three crosses, three domes, and three arches. Looking over my shoulder to be sure no one was watching me, I slipped down the path behind the cathedral to the cemetery. Behind the oleanders, I found the gap in the wall and squeezed through as I had before, pulling my knapsack behind me.

The garden seemed more desolate than when I was last there with Chiyoko. The fish statue on top of the fountain appeared frozen, unable to get out of the entangling vines. I was breathing hard, not from exhaustion, but from fear. Just being in the garden, however, calmed me and made me feel closer to Chiyoko.

I quickly found the pile of bricks we had left at the foot of the wall and searched for the brick that stuck out a little. I pulled on it, but it didn't budge. I took a brick from the pile and hit against the brick in the wall until it came loose.

Did Chiyoko leave me something? I looked in the hole and saw a folded piece of paper in the back. My heart beat faster as I pulled it out and opened it.

> *Nini,*
>
> *I hope you made it home. I worried about you after I left. Soon after that, soldiers came and forced my father to close the clinic. They needed father at the hospital and wanted to send mother and me to Japan. Father agreed to work at the hospital and we were allowed to stay, but I don't know how long. What has happened to you? Please leave a note for me.*
>
> *Your friend, Chiyoko*

I was relieved to know that Chiyoko was still here, that she had not been sent to Japan. But I wondered if she and her mother were living alone and whether they were safe.

I fumbled in my knapsack looking for something to write on. I had only a pencil and a few loose things—but I didn't have paper! *Why didn't I take the time this morning to make sure I could write a note to her?* My hand touched the box in the knapsack.

I pulled out the red box and opened it. There lay the dragonfly, its bulging black eyes staring up at me. The day Chiyoko had given it to me, I hadn't understood the dragonfly as a warning. Chiyoko had been right. Change had come.

I shivered, trying to hurry. I had to get home before they noticed I was gone. I put the dragonfly box in the side pocket with the picture of St. Patrick that Tooner had given me. I rummaged in the knapsack again. Still no paper.

I was desperate to talk to Chiyoko. I could say so much if only we could meet. I took her note and turned it over. I wrote on the back.

I want to see you. Please meet me here SATURDAY 9:00.

I folded the note differently than she had so she would know I had seen it, and put it back in the hole, replacing the brick, not so tightly this time. I grabbed my knapsack and slid back through the gap in the wall.

CHAPTER 5

*R*ushing up the stairs to the apartment, I heard Ma's angry voice. I thought she was yelling at Amah for letting me go. I didn't want Amah to be blamed, but I dreaded Ma's reprimand. Then I heard other voices—men's voices, ones I didn't recognize. The door was ajar. I didn't burst in as I had with Tooner but hesitated this time and peeked around the door.

My little sister Mei-mei was standing in the middle of the Mongolian rug with her eyes wide open, wearing her pajamas. Her hair was sticking out in all directions. Ma was standing nearby, wearing a plain housedress and slippers, her hair loose and hanging down over her shoulders. I wondered why Ma was dressed this way for guests.

"I insist you wait until my husband gets back," Ma said sternly. She was definitely not being polite.

The two men wore dark business suits. One was tall and had his back turned to me, his arms folded across his chest. He was looking at the piano.

The other one, fidgeting with a large set of keys, said, "We don't need your husband now."

I recognized the man with the keys as Mr. Zhou. Da called on him when we needed something fixed in the apartment. Mr. Zhou could get into any room in the building and knew where everything was. He was short and heavy-set with a plump face that hid his eyes. I couldn't tell what he was looking at until he reached down and picked up the brass monkey from the rosewood table and turned it over in his hands.

Mei-mei stared at him. He didn't seem to notice her and put the monkey back on the table. I was glad the letters weren't there.

Mr. Zhou said to the tall man with his back to me, "Did you see this rug?"

The tall man replied with only a grunt.

"I'm sure it's company property," Mr. Zhou said, still jangling his keys.

That's not true! I wanted to shout. I remembered when Ma spotted that rug in a Mongolian peddler's cart. She pointed it out to Da, and he bargained until he got a good price.

"What about this rosewood table?" Mr. Zhou asked.

Suddenly the tall man turned in my direction. He had a narrow face and a stern look. I ducked behind the door and sucked in my breath. Even though I only saw a glimpse of him, I guessed who he was—Mr. Yasemoto! The Japanese officer who had taken over the water company.

My heart pounded so hard I was afraid they would hear it. Mr. Zhou was talking in Chinese and sometimes in Japanese. I wasn't sure Ma understood what he was saying, but it was obvious he was talking about her furniture.

"No. It's worthless," said Mr. Yasemoto.

"Uh, of course. It has a stain. It's worthless," Mr. Zhou agreed. "Do you want to see the other rooms?"

Good for you, Mei-mei, I thought, glad for the time Mei-mei had spilled ink on the brass monkey's spear, staining the table. Then I heard shuffling. I hoped they hadn't seen me and were moving in the other direction, but I didn't dare look.

Right then, a loud cry pierced the air. I peeked around the doorway and saw Amah standing in the hall holding Weilin howling like he'd been pricked with a needle.

Ma rushed past the men and grabbed Weilin from Amah, as if she were afraid they'd take him too. She stood right in the middle of the hall holding Weilin tightly and spoke with more force than I had seen in my mother before, "Get out of my house! I'll tell my husband what you're doing."

Mr. Yasemoto said something to Mr. Zhou that I couldn't hear, and Mr. Zhou spoke to Ma in English. "Husband not work at water company now. We not listen to American wife."

"Get out of my apartment!" Ma insisted.

"You not tell him what to do." Mr. Zhou was shaking his fist. "Not your apartment anymore. It belong to water company."

I heard a clink and glanced at Mei-mei beside the rosewood table. While no one was watching, Mei-mei had stuffed the brass monkey under a cushion on the sofa. The cushion stuck up quite noticeably, but Mei-mei stood in front of it with her arms crossed, just like Mr. Yasemoto.

Weilin let out another cry. I wanted to yell at Mr. Zhou, too, but instead I caught Mei-mei's eye. I held my finger to my lips, *shhh*, to warn her to be quiet. Then I turned and tiptoed down the stairs.

The water company headquarters was in the same compound as our apartment. I found Da in his office talking to a group of workers. Several men were standing around, talking in groups, making angry sounds and harsh gestures.

"You see, don't you," Da was saying to one of the men who was big and heavy like a wrestler. "It's worse than useless to strike now. They have complete control."

"But we don't want to work for the Japanese, and, besides, we can't run the company without you," the heavy man pleaded.

"Zhou will see to it that they have what they need," Da said.

"Urghh, Zhou! I could kill him!" The big man slammed his fist into his other hand.

"Well, it's you who will be killed if you don't watch out," Da said.

"But what will happen to you?" one of the other men asked Da.

"I gave Mr. Yasemoto my resignation letter yesterday. He will do everything he can to blacken my name. I won't be allowed to stay any longer, and he will make it impossible for me to work anywhere else."

"We support you. We should quit too," the big man said while the others nodded.

Da caught sight of me, but he didn't say anything. Instead, he turned and faced the men around the table.

"Listen to me. What you do is up to you," Da told the workmen. "But remember, you have to protect your families, just as I need to protect my American wife and our children. If you quit, how will you support your wife and children? Put your families first."

Da was looking at me now. Then he added, "I have to go. I see my daughter has come with something on her mind."

As Da and I walked out of the room, the men continued talking in heated voices, and the big man began to cry. I had never heard a man cry before and the sound of his sobbing upset me. I couldn't speak at first when Da asked me a question.

"What's the matter?" he asked. "You have come to my office, so it must be urgent. What is it?"

"Mr. Zhou and that tall man—at the apartment," was all I could get out.

"Ah, yes, Mr. Yasemoto. I should have guessed. What are they doing?"

"Taking the furniture."

"He has taken over the company, now he's taking over the apartment, but I didn't expect him to take the furniture too. He wasted no time. Is everyone all right?"

"Yes, but Weilin is crying out."

"I guess he's the only one who can." My father's dark eyes glistened. I couldn't tell if he had been crying too.

Da turned toward the door and put his hand on my shoulder. "Let's make a stop on our way home. I need to make arrangements for tonight."

CHAPTER 6

That night we moved to Auntie Boxin's.

Da had arranged with his rickshaw driver to bring two rickshaws and a cart as well. I rode in Da's rickshaw with Ma and Mei-mei. Amah came in the other one with Weilin and the luggage. Sun rode in the cart that carried the household belongings. The rosewood table was stacked against the back of the cart crowded in against beds, the desk, Ma's dresser, and the sofa. The piano was too heavy, so Ma had to leave it, but she insisted on the Mongolian rug. Sun rolled it up and threw it across the top of the furniture and tied it down. Da oversaw everything, and when we were ready, the rickshaw driver took us first and then went back to get Da.

Auntie Boxin was not my real aunt. I just called her *Auntie* because Da said we should treat her like family. Her husband, Mr. Hansen, had hired Da at the water company. They had been close friends, and Da felt it was his duty to take care of his widow after he died. Mr. Hansen was from Denmark and had come to China to make a fortune. He had fallen in love with a young, beautiful Korean dancer, and that was Auntie Boxin. They had a daughter named Isabella.

Isabella had grown up speaking Korean with her mother, Danish with her father, English and French at school, and Chinese with her amah. Her father had sent Isabella to Europe for her education, but when he got sick, she returned to care for him and now she was eighteen and stuck in China.

After Mr. Hansen died, Auntie Boxin nearly collapsed. Ma said it wasn't the news of his death that made her collapse, but the shock of discovering that he had had a gambling habit. Even with little money, Auntie Boxin stayed in their big house with nineteen rooms. She had to let go of all her servants but one and close off most of the rooms because she couldn't afford to heat them.

The night we moved into Auntie Boxin's house, the wind was howling. I squeezed in close to Ma and pushed Mei-mei to the outside of the seat.

"Careful, Nini," Ma said, without really looking at me. She had many things on her mind. When we settled in, Ma spread a blanket over all three of us and told the driver to go. Mei-mei pulled her knitted cap down over her eyes and ears and leaned toward me for warmth.

We approached Auntie Boxin's house in the dark. The heavy wrought-iron gate creaked when the servant opened it for us. Mei-mei pulled her cap up and leaned out to see where we were. When the driver jerked the rickshaw across the bumpy cobblestones, Mei-mei bounced forward and would have fallen out if I hadn't pulled her back in.

The other rickshaw with Amah and Weilin came through the gate after us and rattled over the bumpy stones. The servant at the gate yelled to Sun to take his cart with the furniture to the servants' entrance.

A sudden draft of wind hit me as I started to climb out of the rickshaw. A loose shutter banged against a window upstairs, and I looked up and saw someone peek from behind a curtain, then close it.

Auntie Boxin stood at the top of the steps. The light coming from inside the house behind her made her look like a tall, dark shadow.

Mei-mei bounded for the stone steps, tripping on the first one. I pulled Mei-mei up, and started climbing the steps, dragging her behind me. Isabella came out the door and headed straight for us, her brown hair loose and wavy, her sweater and skirt bright blue. She took Mei-mei's hand and greeted us. "Come on in. You must meet Sillibub. He's been waiting for you."

We entered a grand entrance hall with a marble staircase on one side and a chandelier hanging above. The servant shut the door; the wind stopped but not the cold.

"Isabella, show the girls to their room," Auntie Boxin ordered.

Isabella headed toward the stairs while Auntie Boxin told Ma they could wait for Da in the drawing room. Auntie Boxin was taller and thinner than Ma. She was dressed in black with a black shawl, her black hair pulled back tight in a bun.

Leading us up the stairs, Isabella said, "Ah, there's Sillibub. I knew he'd come to meet you."

At the top of the staircase was the fattest cat I had ever seen. He was white except for two black feet, and his face was half white and half black. He rounded his back and seemed to grow fatter.

"We call him Sillibub because he looks like a clown," Isabella said.

"He looks like a fur muff," I said.

Mei-mei reached out for him, and Isabella grabbed her hand. "Sillibub doesn't like to be touched," she said. "Leave him alone until he decides he likes you."

I doubted that would happen soon.

We walked down the hall, passing closed doors, until we got to the last one. Isabella opened the door and turned on a small lamp. It didn't do much to dispel the darkness. Heavy drapes covered the windows. I could make out a big bed made of dark wood with a heavy cover and pile of big pillows. It was so high I didn't know how Mei-mei would get into it.

"Your things will be brought up later," Isabella said. "But you might want to keep your coat on." Isabella pulled a stool toward the bed.

Just then the shutter hit the window. The glass in the window rattled and the drapes moved. I shivered and wondered how Ma was going to make it; she was used to a heated house. Maybe she hoped Da could help pay for fuel. Living with Auntie Boxin was not going to be easy.

Isabella must have read my mind and said, "Oh, you'll get used to it. We have a heating system, but, well, the Japanese control the fuel right now. But don't worry, it won't last long." I wasn't sure if she was talking about the cold or the Japanese.

Isabella added, "In the meantime, your amah can make you some padded clothes."

I had always worn padded clothes, but I wasn't sure Ma would like layers of old cloth sewn together like pads under her dresses.

The next morning, Da was gone before we woke. Sun had prepared tea and buns. Da came back and joined us in the dining room—a big, cold room with mirrors on the wall and portraits of people with stern faces. The table was so big we sat only at one end. Da told us what he had heard.

"The Japanese are forcing the foreigners to move into the British district," he began. *How lucky for us,* I thought, because Auntie Boxin's house was already in the British district.

". . . and they have ordered all foreigners to register."

Ma was picking up her teacup when Da directed his comment to her. "You are now considered an enemy alien and you have to register."

Ma slammed down her teacup. "The Japanese are the enemy aliens, not me. I refuse to do it."

"What about me?" I asked. "I'm American, too."

"No, children don't have to register," Da said then turned back to Ma. "I don't see any way out of it. If you don't register, they will track you down. It will only be worse then."

"Well, what do I have to do?" Ma said with resignation.

"You must go to the Empire Hotel tomorrow," Da said.

"Do I go?" asked Auntie Boxin, smoothing her black hair back (although it was already tightly in place). Even for breakfast she was dressed perfectly, and her make-up was just right.

"No, you don't have to register. Japan is not at war with Korea," Da said. "In fact, as a Korean, you can now apply for rations and will receive food and fuel. I will find out where you apply."

Sun brought in bowls of hot noodle soup.

Da went on. "Nini, I want you to go with your mother tomorrow. You might be helpful to her. Amah will stay here and keep Mei-mei and Weilin."

"I can go with Tai-tai," Sun said to Da in Chinese. *Tai-tai* was the polite term for the lady of the house. "When I used to work at the hotel, I knew the manager there. I will talk to him and find out what I can."

Sun used to tell me stories of the Empire Hotel. He said it was the center of the British empire in China, and all kinds of businesspeople stayed there and talked about important things, like where to lay rail lines, and how to get electricity to the foreign districts, and when a dignitary was coming. He helped the pastry chef and said he knew the nationality of the guests by what kind of pastry they ordered: a croissant meant a French guest, and a scone an Englishman.

The next morning Amah woke me early. Sun had soup and rolls prepared for us. I put on my warmest clothes, and Ma was dressed in a tweed suit and wore high heels. I guessed she wanted to make a good impression as an enemy alien.

She put a coat over her suit and said, "This is the heaviest coat I have, but even so, I bet this wind will blow right up my skirt and freeze me to death."

Sun led us along Meadows Road through the middle of the British district. Elm trees lined both sides of the street, and their bare branches stood against a dark, cloudy sky. Each house was surrounded by a wall, some high, some low, some lined on top with shards of glass, some with trellises for vines in the summer, but the walls blocked my view of the houses behind them. I could only see gabled windows, balconies in some, or a tower that rose above the wall.

Sun was ahead of us because he kept walking instead of looking at the houses.

I caught up with him at the entrance to Victoria Park. He was staring at a sign that read, NO DOGS OR CHINESE ALLOWED.

My stomach knotted as I stood next to Sun, confused about what the sign meant. Could I go in the park if I was only half Chinese? What about Sun? Was he no better than a dog?

When Ma caught up, she walked right in. "Follow me. It's faster if we go through the park."

I started to follow, but Sun didn't move.

Ma stopped walking and looked back. "What's the matter?"

"When I worked at the hotel, I never came here," Sun said, still looking at the sign.

"Don't pay any attention to that sign. The British think they are superior to everyone. It doesn't mean anything anymore."

"What about Da?" I asked. "Can he enter the park?"

"Your father never paid any attention to that sign. He's been one of the most important men in the city. All the foreigners need water. How ridiculous if he couldn't enter Victoria Park. But come to think of it, I can't recall that he came here more than once."

"Tai-tai, this way—not be late," motioned Sun.

Ma followed Sun, walking around the park instead of through it. When we got to Victoria Boulevard, the wide street in front of the hotel, we just stood there, staring. The flag of Imperial Japan—a white background and a red circle with lines radiating out in all directions like the sun—was flying from the top of the Empire Hotel.

CHAPTER 7

The Empire Hotel looked like a British castle with a tower in the middle and a turret at each end. It was made of brick and rose five stories high. There were balconies along the front where dignitaries had stood for British parades or celebrations in the past.

"I've never seen a Japanese flag on British property." Ma shook her head in disgust. "And I never thought I'd see one on the Empire Hotel. It makes my skin crawl."

Sun led us across Victoria Boulevard to the entrance of the hotel. People like Ma were milling around. No one seemed to know what to do. Sun whispered to me that he was going around the back to the kitchen to find out what he could. He urged me to stay close to Ma and to watch for things she might not understand.

I was looking around for someone I knew when I spotted Dr. Meyer coming toward us. The last time I saw him was in the summer when I had a bad case of prickly heat and mosquito bites, and when I scratched, I got boils on my legs.

"Ah, Nini, no prickly heat now," Dr. Meyer said as he reached us. Then he turned to Ma. "Brought your interpreter, I see." He was referring to me—not Sun.

Dr. Meyer was Dutch, a beefy man with two chins. He used to love to talk politics with Da.

"Hello, Dr. Meyer," Ma responded. "Yes, Nini's a big help to me. But I'm surprised you're still here. I thought you'd gone back to Holland."

"Holland! Oh, certainly not. The Nazis, you know! Can't go back there. Much better to be here."

"Well, I hope so, but—how's your wife?" Ma asked.

"Haven't you heard? She had a breakdown. When the banks closed, they took our savings. None of the foreign doctors can practice anymore." He pulled Ma close and whispered, but it was loud enough for me to hear. "They got Paul Thompson."

"Oh, no! Is Paul all right?" Ma gripped Dr. Meyer's arm. Ma hadn't seen Mr. Thompson since the day he told us that Pearl Harbor had been bombed.

"He's all right, but they smashed his shortwave radio. Took everything he had."

Dr. Meyer moved on to talk to someone else, and Ma bumped into her British friend, Mrs. Powell, with her puffy white hair and wearing a fur coat.

Ma said she was sorry to hear about her husband's recent death and then added, "But without Mr. Powell, are you going to stay?"

"Of course I am. I was born here," Mrs. Powell said. "My husband, my father, and my grandfather are buried here. I intend to be buried here too. My sons will see to that."

Mrs. Powell continued in a raised voice, "I will register if I have to, but I won't leave!" Mrs. Powell stood erect. "I have more of a right than the Japanese to be here. They will just have to drag me away!"

Beverly Yin, a young American teacher, came up to Ma and didn't even look at me.

"I can't believe I'm here. What a fool I've been," Beverly sighed.

Like Ma, Beverly had married a Chinese man while he was studying in America.

"Why haven't you and your husband gone back to America then?" Ma asked.

"My husband refuses to leave while his parents are still living. But I'm leaving as soon as I can."

"Without your husband?"

"He can come when he's ready. No telling what's going to happen before then."

Beverly moved on and I noticed a commotion at the entrance to the hotel. Japanese soldiers had come out and were barking orders. I pulled on Ma to move, but she wasn't paying attention to me and spoke as if talking to someone else.

"How can she leave her husband? If she wanted out of it, she shouldn't have gotten into it." I nudged Ma again. "I married, I crossed the ocean, that's that. I live with my decision. What are you doing, Nini?"

Ma and I climbed the steps in front of the hotel and entered a large room that was poorly lit. This wasn't what I expected of the lobby of the Empire Hotel. This didn't look like a place where important people had their grand parties and made big decisions. There was no furniture or rugs, no tables with lamps or places to sit. The wood floors were deeply scratched, probably from heavy boots and scraping furniture.

A clatter came from the far side of the room as Japanese soldiers were setting up tables and giving orders. I noticed that each table had a sign for different nationalities. I saw Mrs. Powell heading for the British table, and I nudged Ma into the line that I thought was for Americans.

A soldier with a dark scowl and square jaw barked in Ma's face. I didn't exactly understand him, but I knew Ma didn't, so I answered, "American."

He grumbled at her and pointed to another table they were just then setting up.

Ma moved toward the table, and I followed, but the soldier blocked my way and pushed me aside. Fearful of angering him, I did what he said. I stood away from Ma and the soldiers near a staircase where I could watch what was going on.

I looked around the room in amazement. So many different foreigners, all in one place. Perhaps they were the same people who came here for parties and important meetings, but how different they seemed—usually confident, busy, always in charge of things, now they were confused, frustrated, and being ordered around.

A soldier pushed Dr. Meyer toward a table in the back. At another table I spotted Lillian, the beautiful Polish pianist, who used to come to our house to give Ma piano lessons. I could hear Tooner's voice above all the others. He was at the British line, arguing with the soldiers that he was Irish, not British.

When I looked back at Ma, she was at the front of the line. Her face was stony. A soldier was strapping something on her arm. When she left the table, she didn't even look for me. She just turned and headed for the door.

"Ma, wait for me!" I caught up with her halfway down the steps. Then I could see the black band across her sleeve.

"What's that for?" I asked.

She didn't answer until we got away from the hotel. "All the foreigners have to wear armbands now."

The black strap had a white circle and inside the circle was the bold Chinese character for *America*.

"But why?" I asked.

"It's supposed to humiliate me," said Ma. "But they can't humiliate me by labeling me an American."

Ma was walking fast, but she didn't take the path through the park. She walked around the park the way Sun had.

"Do you know what it means?"

"That I'm American," she snapped.

"No. I mean the character—Chinese and Japanese characters

are the same. It means rice country, the land of plenty," I said. "But it also means beautiful."

She slowed down. "You mean I'm wearing an armband that says beautiful?"

"That's right, in a way."

"Well, this is the first time I've been labeled beautiful." Her gait became more normal, and she tucked the hair that had fallen loose behind one ear. "I guess being labeled *America, the Beautiful* is better than being called *enemy alien.*"

We had a good laugh, and Sun caught up with us as we continued down Meadows Road.

In such a short time, everything had changed. Da had been fired for having an American wife. We had been forced to move, and Ma had to register as an enemy alien and wear an armband identifying her as an American. In the past, my American side had always made me feel safe, but now it was the cause of trouble. *Has the world turned upside down?*

CHAPTER 8

I was required to go to a Chinese school controlled by the Japanese. Nothing about it was like the foreign schools I had been to before. I had to walk a long way to get there. It was in the old British Army barracks that had been abandoned after the British Army left to fight the war in Europe. Some of the windows were broken out, and the desks weren't desks at all but left-over furniture from the barracks.

The principal had a scar on the side of his face. He wasn't a teacher either, just a Chinese government worker who cooperated with the Japanese. All he wanted to do was yell at us in a loud, angry voice, "The foreigners are evil and cruel. They want to take over China. Japan is going to save China from the foreigners."

He said we had to learn to speak Japanese, so a woman came to teach it. All the students were Chinese and didn't want to learn Japanese, so we just stared at the teacher and acted like we couldn't understand her. After the first day, the teacher's face turned red and she left the room. When she came back with the principal, he yelled at us again.

"If you don't learn Japanese, you will become slaves of the Americans. The Americans want to make you their slaves. You must learn Japanese so that you can be strong and victorious over the Americans!"

He walked around the room while the teacher resumed her lessons. She spit out phrases. Repeating what she said, we mimicked her sounds, but we didn't really listen to what she was saying.

At the end of class, the principal lectured us again. He told us terrible stories about how Americans were devils and had horns and how they cut off children's heads. He looked straight at me when he said, *cut off children's heads.*

The room was freezing cold, but I was burning up. I gripped my hands in a fist until my knuckles turned white. The muscles in my throat were so tight I couldn't speak. I started coughing. The teacher dragged me out of the classroom, boxed my ears, and made me stay in the latrine. At least that was better than hearing the principal's lies.

After school, everyone had already left by the time I was allowed to leave. I walked home alone. I wanted to avoid the soldiers, but it was impossible. Soldiers were all over the streets, drinking and laughing. I had never seen them act like this before. Japanese flags were everywhere, and harsh military music was blasting from loudspeakers.

I saw a big banner hanging across the front of a building that read, JAPAN DEFEATS BRITISH EMPIRE. SINGAPORE HAS SURRENDERED!

It made me feel sick. I ran with tears streaming, trying to avoid drunken soldiers and get home as fast as I could.

When I reached Auntie Boxin's house, I saw a man with a cap pulled down on his head, looking up at the house from across the street. He must have seen me because he ran off as I approached the gate. I was surprised to find the gate open. I looked around in every direction.

Was this man watching us? Had he been coming in or going out of the gate? I didn't stop long to find out but ran up the steps and knocked hard on the door.

Auntie Boxin's servant took a long time to answer and then she scolded me. "Why are you making me answer the door? You cause me so much trouble!" I ran past her and straight to the drawing room where we spent most of our time, a small room with a coal stove where we could stay warm.

Ma and Auntie Boxin were at a table near the stove. Ma was reading the newspaper.

"Lies! Lies! Lies!" Ma shouted and slammed her fist on the newspaper.

Auntie Boxin covered her mouth with a handkerchief and didn't say anything.

The Peking Chronicle was the only paper the Japanese allowed to be printed in English. The front page declared in large bold type, JAPANESE VICTORY IN SINGAPORE! BRITISH EMPIRE BOWS IN DEFEAT!

"Does this mean the Japanese are winning, Ma?"

"Of course not!" Ma exclaimed. "That paper is controlled by the Japanese. It's just propaganda. They want us to believe they're winning so we'll give up."

But when Da came home later that day, he told us it was true. The British had surrendered Singapore, just as they had Hong Kong. The US had also lost their positions at Guam and Wake Island.

"Da, are you sure? Aren't they lying?" I insisted.

"No, Nini, it's true. I heard from people I know. We have to trust our friends. That's all we have now."

"The Japanese are winning then?" Auntie Boxin asked in disbelief, muffling her question behind her handkerchief.

"Absolutely not!" replied Ma. "They may win a battle, but they won't win the war."

"But how can you be sure?" Auntie Boxin asked. "My mother was sure Korea would never lose, but look, we lost, and Japan controls Korea."

"We will outlast them. America will come! Just wait."

I was hoping Ma was right about those American planes coming soon. What were they waiting for?

"I am tired." Auntie Boxin pushed herself up from the table. "Where is Isabella? Nini, will you take me to my room?" She was shaking.

Walking Auntie Boxin to her room, I looked toward the front door for Isabella, but I didn't see any sign of her. When she got in bed, Auntie Boxin leaned against the big pile of pillows. Her face was pale.

"Tell Isabella to come see me when she gets in."

Soon after that, I heard Isabella come in and rushed to catch up with her on the stairs. "Isabella," I called to her.

"Nini, don't bother me now," she said, not even looking at me. She wasn't dressed in her usual stylish skirts and sweaters, but in an old dress with a brown jacket. Her usually soft brown hair was covered with a scarf.

"But, Isabella, where have you been? It's already dark outside."

"It's none of your business. I will talk to you later."

"Your mother wants to see you. She is—"

"Leave me alone." Isabella went to her room and shut the door.

The next day when I came home from school, I saw that same man in the cap darting away as I approached. This time the gate and the front door were both wide open. I rushed in and found Amah on the floor holding her head in her hands and moaning.

"What's the matter?" I dropped my knapsack on the floor and knelt beside her. Her hair, usually tied back, had fallen loose. She rubbed her forehead as I helped her sit in a chair.

"Oh, my head," Amah moaned.

"What happened?" I'd never seen Amah like this.

The words came slowly. "A . . . a man . . . I came down . . . down the stairs . . . grabbed . . . hit me on the head."

"Who was it?"

"I didn't see. . . ohhh," she groaned.

"Where did he go?"

"I . . ." She fumbled with her hair, trying to tie it back in a knot.

"You stay here. I'll get help."

I wanted Ma but could only find Auntie Boxin. I told her what had happened, and she cried, "Amah—that useless woman! Did she let him get away?"

"Please, Auntie Boxin. Please come help. Amah is hurt!"

When we reached Amah, she was in the dining room trying to clean up. The room was a mess. Drawers on the side table were opened, and contents were thrown over the floor.

As soon as Auntie Boxin saw the empty drawers, she cried out, "My silver! My silver is gone! My husband brought it from Denmark. It was the finest Danish silver. And the silver tea set too! You let it all go! You fool!"

Auntie Boxin walked over and raised her hand to strike Amah.

Amah cowered as if dodging another blow and moaned like a hurt animal.

"It was not her fault!" I pleaded with Auntie Boxin. "It was a robber! It's not Amah's fault, please!"

"You stupid woman. You could have stopped him." She lowered her hand. "Now you will have to pay for it." Auntie Boxin started coughing. She coughed until her face turned red.

"Come, Auntie Boxin. I'll take you to bed."

The only way to protect Amah was to remove Auntie Boxin. I took her by the arm, and she did not resist.

On the way to her room, I tried to imagine why Auntie Boxin had been so cruel to Amah. Her own servant should have been at the door, not Amah. But her servant must have stayed downstairs, resenting that we stayed here, causing her more work. At any rate, Auntie Boxin had no need of silverware anymore. If it was so valuable, why hadn't she sold it to buy food and fuel and things she needed? What good was her precious silver now!

After the robbery, everything felt different. Da told me robbers knew the Japanese would not punish them for stealing from foreigners. In fact, Japanese soldiers were doing it themselves.

That night I dreamed I was on an abandoned raft. Hands were reaching out as if they were rescuing me, but they were only grabbing at me, trying to take what little I had.

CHAPTER 9

*A*mah jerked my arm. "Come on," she urged, pulling me along the narrow street. A rickshaw sloshed by, splashing muddy water across my legs. "Never mind," said Amah. "Keep moving."

Shops lined the street, little stalls and booths with melons and fruit, live chickens in cages, and fish swimming in pots. Kites, shoes, tea kettles, and incense burners spilled into the street. A merchant reached out for me. Silk cloths hanging from his arms slipped in front of my face, and I lost sight of Amah. A beggar beside a spittoon, one eye bandaged and the other swollen, pure white and blind, leaned forward to grab me, his scrawny brown hand stretching out for my shoulder until his bony finger touched my jacket. I felt a jerk and Amah pulled me forward.

A man passed in front of me carrying a pole across his shoulder with two straps holding a long bundle in bamboo matting. A tiny foot stuck out of the bundle. I jumped back in shock.

"Is that a baby?" I asked Amah.

"Hush," she replied. "He's taking the baby to be buried."

"But I can hear him crying," I insisted. "The baby is alive!"

Amah jerked my arm.

"Nini, wake up. Take Weilin."

Amah was standing beside my bed, shaking my arm.

"Is he dead?" I stammered in my grogginess.

"Hush. You were having a bad dream," Amah said, glaring into my eyes. "Don't bother Tai-tai. She worried all night with Weilin coughing. Here, put him between you and Mei-mei,"

Amah insisted, speaking to me in Chinese as she usually did when Ma wasn't around.

Weilin was wrapped in a bundle of blankets. Amah handed him to me, and I moved to make a place for him in the blankets without waking Mei-mei.

"Now don't wake him. He's finally resting. I'm going to wake Sun. I need his help to make some medicine." Amah turned on the dim light beside the bed and left. I listened to her footsteps padding down the hall.

I seldom got to hold my brother because Amah always had him in tow. His eyes were closed but seemed too small and his ears too large for his head. His skin was pale and his cheeks red, and a little tuft of black hair stuck up over his forehead. His mouth was open, his breathing jerky and labored. He was trying to sleep and sniffle at the same time.

I lay there listening to my little brother breathe while I tried to figure out what route I would take to the hiding place. It was Saturday, and in my note, I'd told Chiyoko to meet me at the garden at 9:00. If she had gotten my message, she'd be there waiting for me. I didn't want to be late.

But how will I go? We had moved into the British district after I left the note for Chiyoko. Japanese soldiers now blocked the streets into the French district. If I could only enter the French district, I was sure I could find my way to the hole in the wall. Da had told me a guard post had been erected at the end of the street near Auntie

Boxin's, but what about the other streets? Surely they couldn't block them all.

I had to see Chiyoko. I couldn't stand the thought of her waiting in the garden without me. Before I had my route fully planned, Amah came back and told me to get dressed and help Sun.

"What time is it?" I asked.

"Never mind what time. Just do as I say!"

Weilin was crying and Amah's full attention turned to him.

I got up and pushed the drapes back. The sky was heavy and gray and gave me no indication of time, only suggesting that night was passing into day. I got dressed quickly in padded pants and a jacket top and went down to the kitchen to help Sun.

Sun was not in a hurry and having trouble getting the stove lit. He told me to keep blowing on the coals while he worked on Amah's medicinal broth. The ashes blew in my face and the smoke made me choke. When Sun had the broth ready, I still didn't have a fire. Sun took over and laughed at me, but I was mad at Sun for being so slow and making me late with Chiyoko.

When Sun finally took the broth to Amah, I slipped out the servant entrance so no one would notice. I wasn't sure what time it was, but it felt late, and I walked quickly.

Auntie Boxin's house was near the boundary between the English and French districts. There never had been a wall dividing the two sides. The English and the French just had an agreement. The signs were in French on one side of the road and in English on the other, and people used to move freely between the two. Now all the foreigners had been forced into the British side, and roadblocks kept traffic from passing from one side to the other. *But there must be many ways,* I thought, *for a person on foot, especially a child, to pass through.*

I checked the intersection at the end of our street, and Da was right—a roadblock had been erected there. I headed to another street and hid behind shrubbery the British had planted to mark the boundary until I could figure out the situation. I stayed hidden until I was sure no one was watching, and then I passed through the bushes into the French district.

I walked quickly, reaching the water company compound. I was afraid someone would recognize me, so I started to turn in another direction. I noticed the gates were closed and no guard was in front. I breathed a sigh of relief and passed on by. I entered the French park and tried to avoid the open areas. The sandbox where the amahs used to bring the children of the foreign families was empty. I walked along the row of benches and fruit trees and was careful to stay hidden by the shrubs and rose bushes.

By the time I reached the shops with the green and white awnings, I was no longer afraid of being in the open. The bakery and the cafe were boarded up. No wonder, I thought, the families who traded there were gone, and so were the owners. Only a few Chinese were out, and no one seemed to take notice of me.

The tall wrought iron gates where the French ambassador had lived were wide open. Trucks were in the drive, and men were shouting orders to others who were lifting heavy furniture. They were busy with their work, and no one seemed to notice me.

The Rue de France had only a little traffic and no policemen or Japanese guards at the platform. There was no sweet potato man to follow this time. But still, I didn't want to cross there, so I went further down.

I was relieved to reach the Cathedral of St. Georges. The three crosses, three domes, and three arches were just as they had always been, but I saw no one going in or out.

When I entered the path behind the cathedral and walked through the cemetery, it seemed to me it was much later than nine o'clock. I easily found the hole in the wall and squeezed through with a sigh of relief. At first the bushes blocked my view of the garden, but I slipped past them until I saw the fountain with the fish sculpture and the abandoned house. But I didn't see Chiyoko. *I'm too late! I missed her.* I was mad at Amah and Sun for being so slow, and at the roadblocks for making me late. Chiyoko must have been disappointed not to find me here. Had she left me a note?

I found the pile of bricks and reached for the brick in the wall that stuck out a little. The brick came out easily and I looked in the hole. There was a piece of paper in the back. I pulled it out and opened it.

Nini,

> *I can't come Saturday. I can't leave mother. My father stays at the hospital most of the time now. Please don't try to come again. It's too dangerous.*

> *Chiyoko*

I fell against the wall and sighed. I was late getting here, but even if I had come on time, Chiyoko wouldn't have been here. Her note made me want to see her even more. It would be so hard for me to come back again.

I pushed the brick back into the hole and kept the note. *I don't care what happens to me. I have to see Chiyoko!* I turned toward the gate and pushed it open.

I had never been in the Chinese part of the city—except once when Da had taken me with him in the water company car with a driver. When I rode in the car with Da, I felt safe, even in the crowded streets, people yelling and selling things, bicycles and trucks and carts all overloaded with too many things. Sometimes the car couldn't move because of the people in the way. A woman with a long pole over her shoulder carrying jugs turned to see who was in the car and her jugs nearly smashed into the window. Children and beggars pressed their faces against the car windows trying to see who was inside. Even with Da next to me, I sunk down in the back seat.

Just outside the gate, I walked past the alley where Chiyoko and I had run the day the soldiers stopped us. The street was quieter than I thought it would be. Most of the doors were closed, and crates and baskets were stacked by the doors. Some women were sweeping with large straw brooms and splashing water from a bucket on the street in front of a doorway. I turned at the first street, remembering what Chiyoko had said.

I knew that her parents' clinic was not far, but I didn't know if they still lived there. Chiyoko had told me the clinic had two entrances—one for the poor and one for everyone else. Her father wanted to serve the poor, she said, but in order to make enough money to do that, he also served those who could afford to pay.

I didn't have to go far before I saw a building marked with a sign written in Chinese and English: *Dr. Mori, Internal Medicine.* The door was plastered with a poster bearing bold black characters that read, *Closed by order of the Emperor of Japan.*

I went around to the other side, and another door was covered with the same poster. A few people were in the street, but I didn't want to bring attention to myself by asking anyone anything.

There must be a third door, I thought. The family apartment would have a separate door from the clinic. In the back of the building, I found an unmarked door. It had no sign indicating Dr. Mori lived there, and it had no poster, either, saying it was closed. I hesitated for a moment, then knocked. I waited and knocked again, this time louder. I knocked once more, and the door opened slowly. I saw two eyes peering out.

"Nini! Is that you?"

"Chiyoko!"

"Quick, come inside!"

I slipped through the door, and Chiyoko shut it behind me. She pulled me into a small entry room where I could barely see her. She held a shawl around her shoulders, and her hair hung loosely, not braided, but combed.

"Nini, you shouldn't have come."

"I had to see you."

"But it's dangerous for you!"

"Are you all right, Chiyoko?"

"I'm all right, but my mother—she's so worried all the time about my father. He has to work at the hospital for days at a time. She has been sick, so I must stay with her and take care of her. Oh, Nini, I miss you so much. I even miss going to school."

"I miss you, too. But you'd hate the school I have to go to—they only teach lies. It makes me so mad. Don't you have to go to school?" I asked.

"I just don't go. No one has noticed. I study with my mother."

"Do you have enough to eat?"

"Oh, yes. Father brings us food from the hospital. Sometimes he even gets rice and fish, but I don't know how long this will last. As long as father is working . . . they have so few doctors, you know."

Chiyoko stopped and looked down.

"It's all right," I said, wanting to comfort her. I knew her father had no choice. And if he refused to work at the hospital, what would happen to Chiyoko?

"How is your family?" she asked.

"We're all right, but my little brother is sick. Amah had to leave him with me this morning while she made some medicine."

"What's wrong with him?" Chiyoko asked.

"I don't know. He wheezes and coughs a lot."

"My father can get medicine. Your mother ought to bring him here and let Father see him."

"Ma can't come here! She has to wear an armband now, and they won't let her through the roadblocks, and even if Ma could pass the roadblocks, I don't think we could get Ma through the hole in the wall, do you?"

We laughed at the thought of Ma in her tweed suit and high heels trying to squeeze through the narrow gap. It felt like old times to laugh, but we quickly grew serious again.

"Do you have enough to eat?" Chiyoko asked.

"Yes, Sun sees to that, and we have Auntie Boxin's rations."

"Who's Auntie Boxin?"

I realized I needed to tell her everything since we parted in the garden, starting with Mr. Yasemoto firing Da, moving to Auntie Boxin's in the middle of the night, and ending with Ma having to register as an enemy alien. While I was explaining the armband, we heard her mother calling from upstairs.

"I have to go, Nini." Chiyoko got up and moved toward the door.

"Can you meet me at the secret hiding place next Saturday?"

"I can't . . ." She paused and turned toward me. She looked like she wanted to say so many things. "I must stay with my mother as long as Father is away. But if I can get away one day, I will leave you a note. Can you do the same, just so I will know you are all right?" Chiyoko pleaded.

"But I want to see you again."

"No, you can't come back here! It's too dangerous."

"I'll come back. I'll find a way, you'll see." I tried to assure her, but I think I was actually trying to assure myself.

"We'll be all right. Just go now and be careful, Nini. Please be careful."

I fought back tears as I stepped out the door and heard Chiyoko turn the latch to lock it.

Sadness filled my heart and tears filled my eyes. I wasn't paying attention when I turned the corner. I walked awhile before I realized I'd gone the wrong direction.

An old man stood beside a wire fence, muttering and looking confused. At first, I thought he was talking to me, pleading for me to do something. Then I saw two Japanese soldiers. One yelled at him in Japanese. I doubt the old man could understand him. The other soldier barked some command, then pointed a rifle at him. The old man looked terrified. He was holding something that looked like a radio in one hand and waving his other hand in protest, begging in Chinese. He dropped the radio, and the soldier lowered his rifle. But the other soldier yelled at the old man and shoved him against the wire fence. The man shook and cried out, then he crumpled to the ground. He lay in a lifeless heap at the bottom of the fence. *What happened? Is the fence electric? How can they treat an old man like this!*

It made me sick to my stomach, and I wanted to scratch their eyes out. I rushed up to the soldier who had pushed the old man and began kicking him, blindly, tears filling my eyes so that I couldn't even see what I was kicking. He yelled to the other soldier.

"Who is this urchin? How dare she attack me!"

"I'll teach her!"

"I hate you! I hate you!" I cried in English, kicking wildly. I was so mad, I wasn't thinking.

"What? What is she saying?" asked the one coming toward me. "Is she foreign?"

"She's a foreign devil!" The one I was kicking grabbed my shoulders.

I realized my mistake. I knew what he was saying because *foreign devil* was what the Japanese teacher called me. Quickly I spoke in Chinese. "I'm Chinese. I'm Chinese! You're the foreign devil!" I kicked the soldier hard in the shin.

"Arugh!" he cried out and let go of his grip on me.

I ran as fast as I could around the corner and past the clinic, not looking behind me. I ran into the alley and through the gate, crossed the garden, and slipped behind the bushes and through the hole in the wall.

CHAPTER 10

Spring 1942

*W*inter passed into spring, and spring brought dreaded dust storms. The wind blew from the Gobi Desert covering everything in a thick film of yellow dust. The dusty sand stung my eyes, stuck in my throat, and thickened my hair. I coughed in the day and wheezed at night. I could not sleep or go out. Mei-mei and I had the flu, and Weilin got worse, then better, then worse, changing each day with the wind.

Ma started coughing and was down most of the time. Amah had more people to take care of than she could manage. Sun kept the meager supplies of rice and meal and a few vegetables in broth for our ailing family.

Auntie Boxin hardly got out of bed during the dust storms. Isabella was kept busy taking care of her mother but sometimes left things to the servant when she went out. When she came back, she didn't have food or medicine, and she was secretive and rude. "It's none of your business" or "leave me alone" was all she would say when I asked where she was going.

Da found work in the sanitation department, but he was fired for no reason. Mr. Yasemoto must have seen to that. Sometimes he made a little money by helping people fix their water problems or by repairing pipes.

The soldiers confiscated all the radios and wouldn't allow people to meet in groups. The only way to get news was one-on-one.

Da would take long walks. Sometimes I went with him. He would talk to one person, then visit another, and pass on what he heard. Da called it "the grapevine" and told me that was how he learned things and knew what was going on. People trusted him, so he learned useful news and passed it on to others.

In the house, Da was restless and paced around. When he couldn't get cigarettes, he became irritable and yelled at me for getting in his way or at Mei-mei for making a mess or at Weilin for crying too much.

The day I came back from Chiyoko's, I went straight to bed. When they found me, I pretended I was sick and had been there all day. But that night I couldn't sleep. I had a terrible nightmare, and when my parents tried to comfort me, they began asking questions. Bit by bit the story came out that I had gone to see Chiyoko *alone*, that I had gone to the Chinese section *alone*, that I had kicked a Japanese soldier.

Ma reacted angrily. "If something had happened to you, Nini, we would never have found you!"

My father stayed calm, but he spoke in that firm voice of his that was worse than yelling. "I know you want to be independent, but you don't realize how dangerous it is."

I was not allowed to go outside alone after that. I felt like my wings had been clipped.

One evening after several weeks inside, Da startled me with an unexpected invitation.

We were in the drawing room. I was reading and Ma was petting Sillibub, who had made his home in her lap. Amah came to take Weilin and Mei-mei to bed and when she reached for Weilin next to Ma, Sillibub hissed at her.

Amah complained in Chinese so Ma couldn't understand her. "Sillibub would be of more use if he would catch the rats in the attic."

"Ha," Da agreed. "Sillibub is useless—just like the Chinese Army, sitting in the lap of luxury while the rats run free!"

Isabella defended Sillibub. "At least he keeps the rats *in* the attic."

Amah left the room with Mei-mei and Weilin. Auntie Boxin decided it was time to go to bed too, and Isabella took her upstairs. When only Ma and I were left, Da turned to me and said, "Nini, how would you like to go to a ceremony with me?"

I closed my book and said, "I'll get ready."

"You don t need to hurry," he laughed. 'It's not till tomorrow and, besides, it has taken a hundred years to get around to it."

"One hundred years! What's the ceremony?" I asked.

"The Japanese are returning the British territory to China."

"Is that how long ago Britain took over China?" I asked.

"Britain didn't take over China, Nini," Ma corrected me. "China was never a British colony like Singapore and Hong Kong."

"You're right, but it's the same idea," Da asserted. "Think of it like this, Nini—what if someone moved into your room. Let's say, he didn't take over the whole house, but he took over your room and brought his stuff in the room and wouldn't allow you to come in. He even put up a sign, NO GIRLS ALLOWED."

At this point, Sillibub slid off Ma's lap and stretched. Da continued, "Let's say Sillibub wandered in the room one day, and the intruder didn't like him and killed Sillibub, and you couldn't do anything about it. How would you feel?"

I didn't really like Sillibub that much, but I knew what Da was saying. I started to say, *I'd kick the intruder in the knees!* but I didn't want to remind Da of what I'd done to the Japanese soldier, so instead

I answered, "I wouldn't let him in my room in the first place!"

Da nodded and said, "Well, I agree. China should never have let them in, but, you see, the British tricked China."

"What do you mean?"

"Well, you see, the British sold opium even though it was against Chinese law."

"What's opium?" I asked.

"It's an illegal drug. The British made the drug in India from poppies and then brought it in ships to China. But the British were not allowed to sell opium in China, so they sold the opium to Chinese traders who took it illegally into all parts of China. When the Emperor tried to stop the illegal drug trade, the British started a war."

Da was fidgeting in his pockets, looking for something. He couldn't buy cigarettes anymore, instead Sun made some from leaves he dried and rolled in thin paper. When Da couldn't find any in his pockets, he started looking around on the table. He found one that Sun had left for him and when he lit it, it popped and crackled. From the way Da pursed his lips and squinted his eyes, I could tell it didn't taste like the cigarettes he used to smoke.

He let out a little cough and blew the smoke in Sillibub's direction. Sillibub made a sniffling noise, shook his head, and moved toward the door.

Da continued. "When the Brits won the Opium wars, they forced China to give them territories as payment. In their own territories, the English could do whatever they wanted."

Then Ma added, "The English weren't the only ones. Japan did the same thing! And the Russians, French, and—"

Sillibub started scratching on the door. Ma got up to let him out, but she continued, "I've always been proud that America didn't do what the European countries did."

"Well, don't be so proud. America got involved too, but that was later, after the Boxer rebellion," Da reminded her.

"But you can't say America acted like the other countries. Why, look at the scholarship you had! America gave back China's Boxer indemnity funds as scholarships. Without that scholarship to study engineering, you wouldn't be the chief engineer at the water company."

"Well, you are right. Without that scholarship, I'd probably be a poor schoolteacher in Shanxi, like my uncles. But don't forget, the money for the scholarship was China's in the first place."

I was getting lost in Da's history lesson and tired of Ma interrupting. Besides, I wanted to know where we were going.

"What about the ceremony tomorrow?"

"The Japanese are going to make a big show. They want the Chinese to think they're on our side, so they're returning the British territory to China. But if you ask me, they're just making themselves look good for returning a room the British took while they're now controlling the whole house!"

"Then I don't want to go." I saw no reason to celebrate that.

"Well, too bad. I thought you might like getting out."

"Oh," I said, "Well, maybe I will."

"I'd like to get out myself," Ma said. "May I go too?"

Da answered, "Sorry, but when you go out, you have to wear an armband, remember. I don't think people with armbands will be very welcome at this ceremony."

The next morning, just as I was putting on my coat, Isabella rushed down the stairs. "Wait. I want to go with you."

Da paused and looked straight at her. "Can you stay with me?"

"Of course, I can!" Isabella responded.

"Well, you must. It will be crowded, and we must stay together. Now, get your coat. It may be cold and windy."

We walked down Meadows Road, the same way Sun had taken me and Ma when she registered. When we got to Victoria Park, the sign that had read, NO DOGS OR CHINESE ALLOWED, was gone. In its place was a poster welcoming the Chinese to the park on behalf of the Emperor of Japan.

I stared at the WELCOME poster. It did not make me feel any more welcome than the old sign. *How would Sun feel?* I wondered. *Would he walk through the park now that the Japanese Emperor welcomed him?*

In the park, bamboo staging had been set up where the gazebo used to be. But where were the benches? The rose bushes? It was just flat, dusty ground with shrubs around the border.

Old beat-up buses pulled up along the street and parked in a row. Someone got out of the first bus carrying a flag and then yelled for the passengers to follow. The bus was filled with Chinese people, looking confused and wearing ordinary street clothes. The person carrying the flag yelled at them, and they followed walking in a straight line behind the flag.

Da led Isabella and me away from the buses and over to the edge of the park where we could see the stage. It was built up high so the crowd could see the people on the stage. Bamboo poles lined the stage and were decorated with banners in bold Chinese characters. Japanese and Chinese flags flew together.

Soon the buses were emptied, and a crowd filled the park. No foreigners were in the crowd. I could see why Da told Ma that people with armbands would not be welcome today.

A drum roll and the blast of a brass horn announced the opening of the ceremony. Men dressed in dark suits with top hats, looking very serious, walked onto the stage.

I was very disappointed. When Da had said *ceremony*, I had expected a festive occasion, but there were no bands or music, no marches or parades, just men with top hats and grim faces.

A Japanese official spoke for a long time. The loudspeaker was garbled, and I doubted anyone could understand anything he said, but I'm sure he said the same things that the principal at school had told us—that the Japanese had come to save China from the devilish foreigners who wanted to cut off their heads. Big applause.

Then a brass horn blew. The Japanese officials unrolled a piece of paper tied in a black ribbon. The leaders of the groups from the buses raised their flags, and the crowd clapped. They raised the flags higher and shook them furiously. The crowd applauded louder.

"What's that, Da?" I asked, referring to the scroll the official was unrolling.

"It's the original deed. The agreement that China signed giving Britain the right to own British territories in China."

The wind had suddenly whipped up, and I couldn't hear him. The flags and banners were flapping wildly. One top hat flew off, and everyone tried to reach for it in the wind. The wind blew harder, and the bamboo poles began to come loose. Chinese workers rushed to hold the poles in place. The loudspeakers went dead. One official fell down and there was a commotion around him.

After a few minutes, things settled down, and the official stood up and held his top hat in the air and bowed. He seemed wobbly and several men helped him off the stage. Everyone cheered. I thought they were cheering because he left the stage, but Da said they were cheering because he wasn't hurt—something blowing in the wind had hit him in the head and he lifted his hat to show that he had been saved from harm.

I wanted to laugh, but just then the wind picked up in a sudden burst. Sand and dust swirled around. I pulled my coat tighter and squinted, covering my eyes with my hand. The crowd began to move in every direction as the wind blew harder and the dust grew thicker.

"Nini!" I could barely hear him, although Da was yelling. "Let's go! Where's Isabella?"

I looked around. She had been with me just a moment ago.

From the corner of my eye, I caught sight of someone—a tall man standing with his arms crossed. A feeling of dread passed through me. *Where had I seen him before?* At first, I was looking straight at him, then he turned around. I recognized him when his back was turned to me the way he was the day he was in our apartment taking our furniture—Mr. Yasemoto! Anger rose inside of me, and I wanted to run up and kick him. Just as suddenly, I could no longer see him.

Then I saw Isabella. She was standing next to a man who had one hand on his cap and another holding his coat closed. *Was this the man who'd been spying on Auntie Boxin's house? Was he the robber?* I wanted to pull her away.

The dust kept stinging my eyes. For a moment I couldn't see anyone. I heard the stage crash, and bamboo pieces scattered in the wind. The Chinese spectators from the buses, no longer following the flagmen in neat rows, were desperately scrambling back on the buses.

Da called again, and Isabella appeared with her head and face covered in a scarf.

I felt Da's hand grab my shoulder. Isabella pushed closely against me. We lowered our heads, held our coats tight, and pushed our way against the wind.

The stage, the banners, the flags all blew away. It seemed the wind blew the whole world away that day.

CHAPTER 11

*S*ummer was as hot and miserable as the winter had been cold and miserable. Every day was hotter than the day before. When I tried to open a window to let in some air, Auntie Boxin fussed that I was letting in the heat. Amah opened the windows at night, but Auntie Boxin's servant closed them again in the day.

Throughout the long summer, I was not allowed to go out alone. I hated being stuck inside the stuffy house and longed to be outside where, if for nothing else, I could breathe and feel the wind on my face.

I worried about Chiyoko. Was she stuck inside too? I went to my knapsack and pulled out the red box. The dragonfly lay still. I stroked its bulging eyes and let my fingers run down the long straight body and across the blue-green wings. *Had Chiyoko been to the secret hiding place? Had she left me a note?* I wanted to tell her what happened to me after I left her—seeing that old man pushed against the electric fence, kicking the Japanese soldier, and my narrow escape through the hole in the wall. But most of all, I wanted to know if she was all right.

One day in the middle of August, I couldn't stand being trapped inside any longer. I needed fresh air. I didn't mean to go anywhere, just to sit on the steps. But the steps were in the hot sun. I opened the gate and moved across the street to the shade of the trees. There was no place to sit, so I walked a little ways farther. The little ways became a little more, and before I knew it, I was walking under the elms along Meadows Road.

When I reached Victoria Park, I could hardly recognize it. The staging had been removed, and nothing had replaced it.

As I stood there staring, a bus pulled up along Victoria Boulevard in front of the Empire Hotel. I quickly hid in the overgrown shrubs at the edge of the park and looked through the leaves. Another beat-up bus pulled up and parked behind the first. They looked like the same buses that had brought the Chinese people to the ceremony I had attended with Da and Isabella, but they were empty.

Japanese soldiers came out of the hotel and began barking orders. I hunched down in the bushes. People followed the soldiers out of the hotel, moving toward the buses. *Who are these people?* At first, I thought they must be Chinese staying at the hotel, courtesy of the Emperor of Japan.

Then I recognized Mrs. Powell. She was dragging a suitcase and wearing her fur coat, even in this horrible heat. The last time I saw Mrs. Powell, she had told Ma she was determined to stay in China and be buried there, like her husband, father, and grandfather. *Was she leaving now? Where was she going?* She looked pale and weak, but she shrugged off a helping hand from a man near her.

My old pediatrician, Dr. Meyer, came out of the hotel. He looked like he needed help. He leaned against his wife unsteadily. I wondered if he wished he had gone back to Holland. The soldiers pushed him along toward the bus.

Following behind them were the two British sisters from school, the ones who pushed Chiyoko and me off the sidewalk. They weren't giggling and poking each other now. In fact, they looked quite stressed. One dropped her bag. It must not feel so good to be British now.

Then I saw Paul Thompson come out of the hotel. I knew it was Paul Thompson because he was taller than all the others. This time, his son, Tommy, was alongside him. Tommy was taller than I remembered. He had a knapsack on his back and another bag over his shoulder. His mother was there too. I was glad the Thompson family had not been hurt after their radio was smashed. They moved to the side and waited while the others filled the bus.

The soldiers shut the doors, shouted orders, and the first bus pulled off. The next bus pulled into its place, and the soldiers began moving more people into it.

I was confused by what I was seeing. Then I heard an unmistakable voice. I wanted to burst out of the bushes, run across the street and up the hotel steps right into his big hairy arms. I wanted him to give my head a buzz and call me his Little Baboon. Tooner was considerably thinner than when I last saw him. His hair was longer and reddish-gray, and his always-trim beard was scruffy.

A guard tried to push him toward the bus. Tooner pulled away from the guard, then he guffawed in his raucous laugh that I loved so much.

Wham! A soldier struck him across the shoulder with a pole. Tooner dropped on one knee, and the soldier whopped him again. There was shouting and confusion. People gathered around and more soldiers rushed over. I saw Paul Thompson move toward them. He didn't say anything and just stood there, hovering over them as if protecting Tooner.

Tooner stood and dusted off his pants. The soldier's pole was still.

Then I heard another sound I knew well—weak at first, then it grew stronger. Tooner was whistling, and almost in Pied Piper style, the others lined up behind him as they moved to the bus.

I had an urge to follow him too, but I pulled back and whispered to myself, "Keep whistling, Tooner. Keep whistling."

I didn't wait to see if I knew anyone else. I was frightened by what I had seen and scared they'd find me and put me on the buses too.

After the second bus pulled away and some of the soldiers went back into the hotel, I crawled out of the bushes.

Once I got home, I sobbed out the scene to Da who asked for everyone to gather in the drawing room. Auntie Boxin sat by the stove with a shawl over her shoulders, even though it wasn't cold, and a fire wasn't lit. Sun stood in the back with Amah holding Weilin. Mei-mei sat on the floor next to Ma's chair. Isabella, who had to be called from upstairs to join us, moved towards her mother.

My father spoke, not in the stern tones I expected, not scolding me, but in a calm, steady voice.

"I heard from the grapevine that the Japanese are rounding up the foreigners. Nini has confirmed what I heard. First, they herded all the foreigners and their families into the British concession. Then they made them register and wear armbands. Then they returned the treaty to China, and now they are rounding up the foreigners and taking them somewhere by bus."

"I was afraid of this," Ma sighed. "Where are they taking them?" She leaned forward, her hand on Mei-mei's shoulder. I noticed for the first time that Ma's hair was turning gray and her face pale and thin, like Mrs. Powell's.

"I heard they were taking them outside the city to a place set up to keep foreigners. No one knows for sure."

Auntie Boxin pulled her shawl closer around her. "But will they take me too?"

"No. Koreans aren't any concern to them. You will be all right."

"But why didn't they take me?" asked Ma.

"I don't know. I heard they were using the names on the relief lists. You haven't applied for any relief, have you?"

"No. We haven't needed any relief. Auntie Boxin's rations have been enough, plus what Sun can get for us."

"Well, you were overlooked for the moment. We don't know if they will come looking for you later. You may be of no importance to them, but we can't take any chances. We will have to keep you hidden."

Da turned to all of us. "Can you be ready tonight? Pack what you need. Sun and I will arrange for everything else."

"What about me? I don't want to leave my house," cried Auntie Boxin.

"I don't want to leave either," Isabella said anxiously. "I mean—I want to stay with Mother."

"You have a choice. You can stay here alone, or you can come with us."

"Tonight?" Isabella asked anxiously.

"Yes."

"But where can we go? They control the city and all the exits now."

Da looked at Isabella, then addressed all of us in a lowered voice.

"I have found a place on the edge of town, in an area that is out near a marsh and open fields. I think we will be able to stay there until . . . until we know more. We'd better move while the soldiers are preoccupied with the foreigners on the buses. We can't wait to see if they knock on the door. Now, move quickly to pack and be ready when Sun calls you. Nini, you help your sister. There's no time to waste!"

Part Two

MORE THAN A YEAR LATER

CHAPTER 12

October 1943

The sun felt good on my face. I was crouching in the tall grasses of the open field, waiting. All I could hear was the whisper of the breeze, swaying white fluffy fronds in the sunlight.

A glint of something bright—purple, gold, and green—caught my eye, and I reached out for it. *Is it alive?*

Grasshoppers fed on the wild millet growing in the field. Mei-mei and I had watched them swarm and fly away in great numbers, but I had never held one in my hand. I didn't know their wings were so beautiful. The grasshopper was dead and his middle had been torn open. Probably a snake or an insect had killed the grasshopper and been scared away before eating it. Even the littlest creatures were hungry these days.

His insides were purple and green and shiny, the small grains in his stomach packed tight and undigested.

At least somebody's belly is full, I thought. *Too bad you didn't get to enjoy your meal.*

I was putting the grasshopper back in the grasses to be someone else's meal when I heard them coming. Three boys were beating a path toward me through the tall grasses, laughing as they flattened a trail in their wake.

For over a year, we had lived near this open field on the outskirts of the city. Here I could be outside all day. Mei-mei and I often played in this field. Twin brothers, Ying-wei and Ying-jun, who lived nearby, had played with us at first—playing hunters, building forts, and hiding to surprise each other—but then an older boy named Tai turned them against us.

I jumped up and hollered, "Mei-mei, here they come!"

Mei-mei knew how to use her small size to our advantage. When the boys came running and laughing, they didn't see her hiding in the grass. One of the twins tripped over her, and then the other, and Tai fell on top of them. Mei-mei jumped up and ran as fast as she could. She caught up with me, stirring up a swarm of grasshoppers as we headed to the edge of the field.

"That'll teach 'em!" I said, out of breath and delighted with outwitting them.

We walked home along the road on the edge of the field. When we pushed open the gate and entered the courtyard to our house, we saw the price of our victory. While we had been hiding in the field, the boys had come and smashed the mud village we had built with Da.

We moved to this house the night we left Auntie Boxin's. It was plain—the color of mud itself. I wasn't happy when I first saw it, but I liked the fact that Auntie Boxin and Isabella lived upstairs, and we lived downstairs. And most of all, I liked being next to the field and the fact that I could be outside.

Ma, however, never went outside. She tried to stay out of sight and at first was afraid to even look out the window—afraid that someone might see her narrow face and brown hair and send her off with the other foreigners. But it had been over a year, and no one had come looking for her.

Da kept a watch on things. He walked around and talked to people, as he had before. He always had news when he came home, and I listened when he talked to Ma. The Japanese were in full control in the city now. Those who collaborated with the Japanese were able to get food and things that the other people could not. Da was furious when he heard that Mr. Zhou was a big shot in the water company and lived in our former apartment.

Inside our courtyard, we had created our own world. There was no garden, only dirt, and when it rained, rivulets formed in the mud. One day the previous summer, we had started to build little mud houses along the rivulets. The houses grew into a village.

Mei-mei and I convinced Da to help us build our village. He had more time on his hands, and, besides, he knew how to build things. He helped us control the water flow by building a dike along one rivulet that we could open and close, depending on how much water we wanted to come through. We pretended to let in a lot of water and flood the village, or we could stop the water in time and save all the villagers.

I made roads and built mud houses. Mei-mei rolled the mud into balls and made little people with sticks for arms and legs.

What's that?" Da asked her one day.

"It's *ni-ren*," Mei-mei answered. "We need people for our village, don't we?"

"Ahh," said Da. "Do you remember the *ni-ren* maker from the market?"

Ni-ren meant mud men. We used to watch the Chinese artist, a *ni-ren* maker, at the marketplace in the French district, working his hands fast, mixing clay and water. People would gather around and watch until he had quite a crowd. He would make a figure that looked like someone in the crowd, like a French policeman. If the policeman bought it, everyone would clap and the *ni-ren* maker was happy.

Mei-mei rolled balls into round shapes and put them in groups, like children playing together. She asked Da to help her. He made a man pushing a cart and another fishing. Mei-mei found a twig to use as a fishing pole. Da made a bridge to put the fisherman on with his fishing pole hanging over the water, and Mei-mei clapped with delight.

When we pushed open the courtyard gate that day, it looked as if a typhoon had swept through our mud world. The houses were smashed, and the little people were stomped into the ground or scattered all over. The bridge with the fisherman was not to be seen. No force of nature had caused this destruction. I knew immediately it was the meanness of the boys, their big feet stomping, smashing, flattening our village. While we had been hiding in the field, no one had been watching out for our beautiful mud world.

I wanted to run out to the field and knock their heads together, but instead, I stormed inside the house, snarling like a mad dog.

"Da! Ma!" I yelled. "Our world is destroyed!"

"The boys smashed our village!" Mei-mei joined me in denouncing the boys' attack.

"You can build it again," Ma said.

"But we can't—not that one!"

"You can build another one . . . and make it even better."

"Oh, Ma. You are always saying things like that. But we can't make things better. Where is Da?"

"He's out. Go take those clothes off. You'll make me sneeze."

Dust and pollen made Ma sick. It seemed to me, however, it wasn't what we brought in that made her sick but the fact that she couldn't go out.

"Mei-mei, you too," Ma said urging us to the kitchen. She wore her padded jacket and pants even though it wasn't cold. "Tell Amah to shake the dust off your clothes. You'll be the death of me yet."

CHAPTER 13

"Amah, Amah, take my clothes off," Mei-mei called out as we entered the kitchen. "Ma's going to sneeze."

Amah didn't answer. Her back was turned to us. Even from behind her I could tell something was wrong.

"Are you crying?" I asked.

"Not crying," she mumbled. "Sun should do this work."

Da had let Sun go because he couldn't afford to pay him. We all cried when Sun left, and Mei-mei clung to his legs, begging him to stay. He found another job as a cook for someone who could afford to pay him. He promised to come back and check on us, but we hadn't seen him in more than a year. We all missed Sun terribly, but it was Amah who missed him the most.

Amah had to take over the cooking, and she complained that she was a nanny, not a cook. At first Ma tried to help with the cooking, but the coal stove was hard to manage and the iron pot too heavy. And besides, Ma only knew how to cook with things we didn't have, like eggs, milk, and butter. Amah couldn't do what Sun used to do, but she could handle a coal stove and knew how to manage without things.

"Oh, goodie! Dumplings!" Mei-mei squealed.

"No, not dumplings!" Amah snapped. "No flour—no dumplings."

I remembered how Sun made the best dumplings. He'd roll the dough into thin circles, fold it over a little bit of meat stuffing, then pinch the edges into a half moon shape. But Amah's dough didn't look like Sun's. When she pressed the sides, it fell apart.

"Then what are you making?" Mei-mei asked.

"Get out of kitchen now. Go take your clothes off," she ordered us in English.

I stared at the crumbling dough. "Those aren't dumplings," I said. Then Amah let out a deep sigh and put her hands to her face.

"I miss my home," she sobbed into her hands.

Amah had left her family in the countryside years ago. Da said she stayed with us because she had nowhere else to go. She had always worked for foreigners in the city, and now the foreigners were all gone, except for Ma. He promised to pay her when the war was over and told her that at least with us she had food and a place to live. I had never heard her mention home before.

"Oh, Amah," Mei–mei said soothingly, putting her hand on Amah's arm. "We are your home."

"When I was a little girl, my mother told me stories, and we ate moon cakes. I want to make moon cakes, but there is no flour—just ground up corn!" Amah dropped her hands to the table and stared at what she was making.

"That's all right, Amah. We can pretend to eat moon cakes," Mei-mei smiled.

"Why are they called moon cakes anyway?" I asked.

Amah burst into tears. A strand of her hair fell across her face. Mei-mei coaxed her onto the bench next to the wall and then patted her knee. When she quit sobbing, Amah sniffed, "You don't even know what moon cakes are! You are not Chinese."

"But we *are* Chinese!" I insisted. "Da is full Chinese. Mei-mei and I are half Chinese."

"Da will tell us what moon cakes are," Mei-mei said.

"No, he won't!" Amah snorted. "He lived in foreign world. He forgot Chinese ways."

"Well, if our father can't tell us, then you tell us," I insisted.

"You won't understand. It was a long time ago in China, when other foreigners were here." Amah used a Chinese word for foreigners that meant they did not come from across the ocean.

"What foreigners?" Mei-mei scowled, picking up on Amah's dislike of foreigners.

"Mongol people from the North."

"When did they come?" I asked.

"It was a hundred, maybe a thousand years ago."

"And you still remember it?" Mei-mei's eyes grew big.

Amah glared at her and went on. "The Mongol people took over. Chinese people were unhappy then. No one wanted foreigners to rule us. Then Chinese leaders came up with a bright idea at the time of the Moon Festival."

Mei-mei interrupted again. "Moon Festival?"

"See, you don't know anything! This time every year when the moon gets big. Like tonight."

"Tonight is Moon Festival?"

"No, there is no festival now. Japanese soldiers took it away. But the soldiers can't take the Moon away. Tonight it will rise big and round." Amah's voice grew softer, and she began talking in Chinese, as if her memories were in Chinese. We understood her because she had always spoken to us in Chinese, and sometimes Da did too.

"When I was a little girl and the Moon hung in the sky like a big golden lantern, my mother would point to it and tell me the story of the beautiful Lady in the Moon."

Amah lifted her hands into the air with her fingers, making a circle as if she were looking at the Moon.

"I could see Chang-o dancing on the surface of the Moon. You see, she couldn't get away. Do you know why?"

"No, why?" we chimed in unison.

"Because she swallowed the Elixir of Immortality."

"The what?" Mei-mei asked.

"That means she never dies," Amah explained, enjoying our ignorance now.

She began talking faster. "You see, she was the wife of the magic archer, Yi. He could hit anything with his arrows. In fact, he could fly on the wind faster than his own arrows and catch them and bring them back." Amah looked past Mei-mei and continued.

"Long ago the earth had ten suns and it was too hot. The emperor asked Yi to help. Yi used his magic arrows to shoot down nine suns. One sun was enough for light and warmth. As a reward, the emperor gave him the Elixir of Immortality."

"Did he drink it?" Mei-mei gulped, as if waiting for the liquid to go down her throat.

"No, his wife found it and swallowed it in an instant."

"That's not the end of the story, is it?" I prodded, not wanting her to stop.

"No, no, no. His wife began to float. She floated up and up, rising in the sky, past the white clouds, and on up until she reached the moon. And there she still lives. If you look tonight at the full Moon, you can see her. Sometimes you can see her white rabbit too. But that's another story."

"Does Chang-o eat moon cakes?" Mei-mei asked.

"Oh, no, she doesn't need to eat."

"Well, what about the moon cakes?" Mei-mei looked puzzled.

"You didn't tell us about the Mongols, did you?" I reminded her.

"Ah, yes," said Amah. "You see, the Chinese leaders came up with a clever plan. They wanted to get rid of the Mongol people. When the full Moon came around, the leaders ordered cakes to be made in the shape of the Moon, round and puffy. They slipped a message inside the cakes. Only the Chinese people ate the cakes, so they read the message and knew the plan. On the night of the full Moon, all the Chinese attacked and overthrew the Mongols. So, we always celebrate with moon cakes.

"What about the white rabbit?' Mei-mei asked.

"No more stories. Get your clothes off!"

CHAPTER 14

*M*oonlight streamed in the window that night, falling across Mei-mei's sleepy round face. Was Mei-mei dreaming of Amah's stories? Was she dreaming of the magic archer and the Lady in the Moon, or the Mongols and moon cakes?

My thoughts came rushing back as my stomach growled. Amah's crumbling corn meal hardly tasted like a moon cake, and with only some thin soup, it didn't feel like a festival at all.

If the Chinese long ago had had crumbling corn meal, I thought, *they couldn't have hidden messages inside.* What if they couldn't use the moon cakes to hide messages, then could they have defeated the Mongols?

It wasn't the moon cakes that defeated the Mongols. *It was their clever thinking!* They used whatever they had. If they didn't have moon cakes, they'd use something else, even corn meal or mud.

Mud? Yes, mud!

That gave me a clever idea.

"Wake up, Mei-mei! Wake up!" I shook Mei-mei until her eyes fluttered and she gazed sleepily at me.

"I have an idea! Listen," I whispered in her ear, but her eyes shut again.

I was so excited about my plan that I couldn't sleep. I got up and went to the window.

I could see over the low wall and into the field beyond it. The grasses were calm and still, and the moonlight made everything look like colorless day. Then something moved.

Is it a shadow? No. It's a man. I couldn't see his face clearly, because he wore a cap, but he looked like the man I saw watching Auntie Boxin's house that day now long ago. *Was he the robber who stole Auntie Boxin's silver? Was he the same man I saw with Isabella in the dust storm?*

I ducked, hoping he wouldn't see me. When I peeked again, he was gone. I crawled back in bed. *Who is this man? Is he spying on us?*

Maybe I had imagined it. Maybe I was so full of Amah's stories that I had imagined a man in the moonlight. I pulled the covers up to my chin and tried to sleep in the eerie light.

The next morning, Mei-mei and I started on my plan as soon as we went outside. Ma thought we were rebuilding our mud world, but we had a different idea. We took small amounts of mud and rubbed them round and round until we had a hard ball. We placed the balls in piles. We knew we had to be ready by the afternoon when the boys were likely to return.

We put as many balls as we could in our pockets. Mei-mei went first. She was just tall enough to pull herself up onto a low wall next to the house. With one foot on the wall and the other on the trellis, she was able to climb up to Auntie Boxin's balcony. From there she held on to the vines that grew on the side of house and shimmied onto the tile roof.

I went next. My full pockets got in the way and made it hard to climb. Before I reached Auntie Boxin's balcony, I grabbed some vines. One of them broke, and I almost fell, dangling and reaching for the trellis.

"Mei-mei!" I cried, trying to keep my voice low enough so I wouldn't wake Auntie Boxin from her nap or make Amah come out and see what we were doing.

Slowly I was able to get my footing on Auntie Boxin's balcony and use the trellis to climb onto the edge of the roof. We scooted across the tile roof on our bottoms, to the side of the house that faced the courtyard.

We emptied our pockets and piled the balls on the ledge beside the roof gutter.

We had more balls to bring up, but I didn't want to climb down again, so I told Mei-mei to go.

"I can't carry all those balls!" she protested.

"Here," I said. I took off my sweater and gave it to her. "You can fill it with balls. Just tie the sleeves together and bring it back."

"I can't climb up carrying that."

"I'll drop a vine over. You can tie the sweater to the vine, and I'll pull it up."

She scurried down again and while she was filling the sweater with the remaining mud balls, I broke off several pieces of vine from the side of the house and tied them together until I had a long rope.

When she got all the balls in the sweater, she yelled, "What do I do now?

"Tie the sleeves together and then wrap it with the vine," I tried to whisper and holler at the same time.

"I don't know what you mean," she complained.

"Do I have to come down and do it myself?"

I dropped one end of the vine and held the other.

She wrapped her end of the vine around the sweater and tied it to the sleeves, then asked, "Now, what do I do?"

"Nothing. I'll pull it up."

I pushed against the tiles with my feet and pulled the vine one hand over the other. As the bundle got halfway up, it began to sway in the air, and then started spinning. Balls started falling out.

"Watch out! It's falling apart!" I called to Mei-mei, but she had already started scrambling up the trellis again. I kept pulling slowly until she reached me just in time. Grabbing the vine with me, we pulled the unraveling bundle over the edge and fell back on the roof.

"Whoa, that was close," I said as I untied the sweater. We stacked the balls along the edge. I was chilled from the wind and glad to put my sweater back on. Mei-mei tried to wipe it off with her muddy hands.

"Stop it! That only makes it worse," I said. But the sweater didn't matter. Our plan was ready. We both rubbed our hands together, then grinned at each other.

The boys were arguing but quit talking when they got to the gate. Tai went first and entered the courtyard. He was carrying a long stick. He quickly slid next to the gatehouse where coal used to be stored. He motioned with the stick for the twins to enter, directing them to stomp on what was left of the village.

Ying-wei entered the gate, then stopped. "What?"

Ying-jun was right behind him and peered over his shoulder. "It's gone!"

Tai shoved the twins aside and moved in front of them.

"Go!" I whispered, and we pelted them with a shower of hard mud balls. Mei-mei and I threw as fast as we could, handfuls at a time.

"What the—?" Tai tried to bat them off with his stick.

"Watch where you're slinging that stick!" Ying-wei shouted.

"Ouch! Stop hitting me." Ying-wei yelled and he pushed Tai into the coal bin. "Let's get out of here!" he shouted at his brother. He tried to open the gate, but the latch stuck.

Ying-jun scuttled over the wall. Ying-wei scrambled over him, falling to the ground outside the wall. Tai followed, stepping on Ying-wei. All three ran toward the field and disappeared in the tall grasses. From the roof, I could see the white fronds waving behind them in a long, jagged path through the field.

"They won't bother us again," I said, grinning at Mei-mei.

"There's one more," she said, pointing to a figure fiddling with the latch. As the gate opened, we let loose again with the few mud balls we had left.

Then we heard a stern, unmistakable voice.

CHAPTER 15

*B*a was furious, not because we pelted him with mud balls, but because we had climbed on the roof.

"If you fell and broke a leg, where could we go for help? You know we can't take you to any hospital."

Amah was mad about the dirty sweater. "We have no soap," she said. "And besides, I have too much to do already."

Ma was upset because instead of rebuilding the village, we had turned the mud into weapons.

"The war has gotten into you. You are acting just like them." Ma glared at me. "Don't you see? You have made enemies when you need friends."

So what? I thought. *They started it.*

Deep down I knew Ma was right. Ying-wei and Ying-jun had been our only friends before Tai started acting like a bully and turned them against us. They pretended to go along with him, but I knew they wanted to play in the field with us like we had before. I knew they would never play with us now.

The weather turned cold and rainy, and even if we weren't being punished, we all had to stay inside.

One day Da decided it was time for me to learn to write Chinese. I could speak Chinese, of course, and read some of it, but I had never studied calligraphy. Da got a brush and an ink stone from the desk and asked if I was ready to begin. I sat on the floor beside the low table and watched him. He took a stick of black ink and mixed it with a little water, rubbing it back and forth on the ink stone until he had a pool of black ink in the stone.

Sitting on his knees on the floor with the paper in front of him, Da dipped his brush into the ink, just so.

"You start from the top," he said and stroked down in one swift movement.

He followed that stroke with another one, starting mid-way down and going to the right.

"Do you know what that means?" he asked.

"Of course, I do. It means *man*."

"What about this?" He made two of the same markings, one beside the other.

"Two men," I answered quickly.

"It means *follow*. One man following another. Now, Miss Know-It-All, you do it. Knowing what it means and doing it are two different things," he said.

He slid the paper in front of me and handed me the brush. I dipped it into the ink and made a big blob on the paper.

"No, no, no. Too much ink! Just a light dip is all you need."

I tried again. This time I barely dipped the brush in the ink and made a stroke.

After awhile Da got up and let me work alone. I was concentrating and didn't notice that Weilin was watching me from the sofa next to Ma. Before Ma could stop him, he climbed down and squatted near me. Mei-mei, seeing the empty spot next to Ma, climbed up on the sofa.

"Ma, can you tell me a story about a girl like me?" Mei-mei asked.

"Like you? Well, there's no one just like you, you know."

"I know, but sorta like me."

"Well, I know one about a little girl whose name is Gretel," said Ma, getting settled with Mei-mei on her right side.

I already knew the story of *Hansel and Gretel* so I didn't have to listen, but I wanted to hear the part about the witch.

"Hansel and Gretel lived with their father and step-mother in a small cottage on the edge of a big woods," Ma began. "Times were hard, and they had little to eat. One night while Hansel and Gretel were in bed, very hungry, they overheard their parents talking."

Weilin moved closer to the ink stone. "No, don't mess with the ink! This is mine." I scolded him.

Ma went on. "When the children overheard their step-mother planning to take them deep into the woods and leave them there, Gretel began to cry."

"Ma!" I burst out. "Weilin is bothering me!" I moved my paper and the ink stone from the floor to the rosewood table.

"Come here, Weilin. You can be Hansel," Ma said, urging him up to the sofa. She pulled him into her side opposite from Mei-mei.

"Hansel went outdoors and picked up some pebbles and filled his coat pockets with them and went back to bed. The next morning, when the step-mother took the children into the woods—"

"Ma, get to the good part!" I interrupted impatiently.

"Be quiet, Nini," Mei-mei said.

Just when Ma was about to get to the witch and the gingerbread house, Mei-mei pestered her with questions. "Was the roof made of gingerbread? What did it taste like? Was it like Sun's cakes?"

Ma laughed and said, "Ah, yes, you remember Sun's cakes, don't you? You must be as hungry as Hansel and Gretel. What do you think they did?"

"They ate it!"

"You are right! Hansel broke off a piece of the roof and ate it. Gretel chipped out a piece of the windowpane and ate it."

Mei-mei sat up. "Did they eat the whole house?"

"Not so fast. Before they could get that far, they heard a creaky old voice, 'Who is nibbling at my house?'"

Just at that moment, Auntie Boxin opened the door from her apartment upstairs. "May Isabella and I come in?"

Auntie Boxin and Isabella stayed upstairs most of the time and seldom came down. *Why did they have to barge in just when Ma was about to get to the good part?*

Da replied, "Of course, please come in."

"But, Da," I protested.

He glared at me. Ma called to Amah to bring some tea, and I knew that meant Auntie Boxin would stay for a while. Ma welcomed her to sit in the chair next to the sofa.

Auntie Boxin was holding her black shawl with one hand and a handkerchief in the other. Isabella came alongside her and helped her. Auntie Boxin moved so slowly that I had made five bold characters by the time she was seated.

Amah brought a tray with cups of hot water. We hadn't been able to buy tea for a long time. She set the tray on the rosewood table. As she turned to leave, she tried to assist Auntie Boxin with her chair, but Auntie Boxin pushed her away. I knew Auntie Boxin was still mad at Amah. She hadn't talked to her since the silver was stolen.

Isabella thanked Amah, reached for a stool, and sat next to her mother.

Auntie Boxin turned to my father and asked, "Have you heard anything new?" She didn't even apologize for interrupting. My brush made a big blob on the paper.

"No, there's been no change. The Chinese army is trapped in the interior. The Japanese control the cities. We hear gunshots or explosions sometimes from outside the city. Those must be attacks by the Eighth Route Army. They seem to be the only ones fighting the Japanese."

Auntie Boxin coughed and held the handkerchief to her mouth. Isabella put her arm around her mother's back until she quieted. "Do you want some tea, Mother?"

"Yes, please."

Isabella poured a cup of hot water and handed it to her mother, and then she turned to Mei-mei.

"Did we interrupt your story, Mei-mei?" Isabella asked.

"Yes. Gretel is eating a house." Mei-mei sounded like her own meal had been interrupted.

"Oh, Hansel and Gretel! My father used to read that to me. When I was in Denmark with him, we went to see the opera."

"You saw the opera *Hansel and Gretel*?" Ma exclaimed, shifting both Weilin and Mei-mei at her side and turning toward Isabella.

"Why, yes, it's quite popular in Europe."

"I love that music, especially the evening prayer that Hansel and Gretel sing when they're alone in the woods."

"Oh, yes!" Isabella clapped her hands in front of her chest. "My father and I used to sing it before I went to sleep."

"Could you sing it now?" Ma asked.

"I'm not sure."

"Why not?"

"It will bring back such memories of my father."

Then Isabella closed her eyes and pressed her hands together as in a prayer and began to sing in a soft voice:

When at night I go to sleep
Fourteen angels watch to keep
Two my head are guarding.
Two my feet are guiding—

"What are angels?" Mei-mei interrupted. "Are they like the Lady in the Moon?"

Isabella stopped singing and laughed. "No. You can't see angels, but they are always nearby. Angels protect you, keep you from harm, and sometimes help you when you're in trouble."

"Oh," said Mei-mei. "I'm always in trouble. I hope I have lots of angels."

"I'm sure you do," Isabella assured her.

"May I sing it with you?" Ma asked.

"Of course!"

Isabella continued the song and Ma joined in.

"Two are on my right hand,
Two are on my left hand,
Two who warmly cover,
Two to wake at dawn do hover,
Two to guide my steps to heaven!"

"It makes me sad. I remember hearing you singing with your father at bedtime," Auntie Boxin interrupted. She touched one eye with her handkerchief.

My calligraphy lesson was finished. Auntie Boxin and Isabella had completely taken over. I wiped the brush and dropped it on the paper. There was no use in trying to concentrate anymore, so I got up and walked over to the window with my back to the rest of them. For the first time that day, I felt trapped inside. I stared out the window to the field beyond the wall, wondering when I could go outside again. Then I saw something . . . or someone.

"Stop!" I turned around. "Hide! Ma, hide quickly!"

Everyone stared at me, stunned. Isabella jumped up, knocking over the teacups, spilling water across my calligraphy. She rushed outside, leaving the door wide open with the cold air blowing in. In a moment she was back, standing at the door with the man I had seen many times before. The spy was standing at our door!

CHAPTER 16

I stared at the spy. I had seen him at Auntie Boxin's house, running away after the robbery, at the ceremony in the dust storm, and last night in the moonlight, but I had never seen him up close. He was younger than I thought. He looked more like a student than a robber or a spy. He took off his cap and held it in his hands. His hair was full and thick. He raked his fingers through it, as if trying to look neat. He had a square chin and sharp cheekbones. He wore loose black pants and a jacket.

Isabella was flushed. She looked around the room. No one moved, then she spoke directly to Ma.

"Auntie," she said, at first hesitatingly and then with boldness. "Auntie, this is Zhao Ren. He . . . he's our friend. You see, he has been protecting you."

"Protecting me?"

"What?" I shouted. "But he's a spy!" I wanted to add, *and a robber*!

"What do you mean, Nini?" Isabella exclaimed, adding, "Well, he is a spy . . . in a good sort of way. But let me explain." Isabella looked at Da, as if asking permission.

"Please, come in," Da said to Zhao Ren. Isabella and Zhao Ren stepped inside and Da shut the door behind them.

"Here, have a seat," Ma said, motioning to the sofa. She got up and moved to the other side of the room next to Da.

Weilin climbed off the sofa and walked over to Zhao Ren. I guess he wanted to see a spy up-close. Zhao Ren looked down at Weilin, then reached out his hand, and they walked to the sofa together.

Isabella and Zhao Ren sat down, with Weilin scrunched between them and Mei-mei scooting close to Isabella on the end.

I stayed near the window, keeping a distance.

"You see," said Isabella. "Zhao Ren has been watching out for us."

"Let me explain, Isabella," Zhao Ren said in English. "Everyone, please, I feel I know you, but you don't know me."

"You see," Isabella kept going. "He's a member of the—" Auntie Boxin coughed.

Zhao Ren interrupted, "Let me explain, Isabella." He seemed hesitant to say more and looked at me, then at Mei-mei.

Da must have guessed the cause of his hesitation and said, "It's all right to speak in front of the children. They need to know too."

"Let me start then by assuring you, Nini," Zhao Ren began, "that I meant no harm to you or your family. I knew you saw me, but I couldn't talk to you or tell you why I was there." His voice was soft and kind, but I still didn't trust him.

"Why did you steal Auntie Boxin's silver then?" I asked.

"I didn't steal the silver. I saw the robber run out of the house and I followed him. You must not have seen him and assumed I was the robber."

Isabella interrupted this time. "Zhao Ren found out who the robber was. Later I learned our servant had let the robber into the house. They were both stealing the silver and other things. I told your father and he fired the servant."

Zhao Ren looked at my parents and continued. "I have been watching you for nearly two years. I am part of . . . well, let me go back a bit. You see, when the Japanese attacked China, I was a student at the university. Many of my friends and professors left the city. I helped them pack up books—they took as much of the library as they could. They even took printing presses and equipment. They carried everything they could on their backs and in carts, carrying them over the mountains."

"I know many people who left then," said Da.

Zhao Ren went on. "They joined students and teachers from other cities and moved farther inland."

"Yes. They moved to areas outside of Japanese control," Da said.

"We call it the Free Zone. From there they sent information to the occupied areas—to those of us in the cities on the coast. I wanted to go with them, but some of us had to stay here. We listen and watch and send the news we hear to them."

"Yes, I know. That's what I call the grapevine," Da said. "It's how I get information when I walk around and talk to people."

"But that is not all," interrupted Isabella.

"I've been watching out for your family," Zhao Ren went on. "I stay informed of any threats and watch to see who comes around your house. I'm in touch with others in case there is trouble."

Isabella blurted, "I am too, Mother. I am with Zhao Ren and the others. I, too, joined the underground resistance. We are secretly working against the Japanese to free China."

"Isabella, how could you? It's too dangerous. You could be killed! Why haven't you told me?" Auntie Boxin protested.

"I'm sorry, Mother, I know I left you so many times and couldn't explain where I was going. But I had to do something. When I was in Europe, I saw the Nazis taking over. I didn't want the same thing to happen here with the Japanese. I was so distressed at what was happening. When I met Zhao Ren, well, he showed me how I could help and—" She looked at him with admiration.

"Let me explain further," he said. "There is urgency now. The Free Zone is in crisis. The Allies have created a supply route into China through Burma, but the Japanese have attacked it, and no supplies are getting through now—no weapons or food. The peasants are exhausted. They have given everything they have to the army. I need your help now."

"But how can we help? We have nothing, hardly any food ourselves," Ma said with despair.

Auntie Boxin began coughing and couldn't stop. Isabella looked distressed. "Do you want me to take you upstairs?" she asked her mother.

"Yes. I can't—" Auntie Boxin tried to stand but slumped back into the chair.

Ma turned to me. "Nini, help Auntie Boxin. Isabella needs to stay here."

But I wanted to stay and hear what else Zhao Ren had to say. I looked at Auntie Boxin hoping she would not insist. But she only coughed again, and Ma glared at me. Da helped Auntie Boxin stand and motioned to me. I grudgingly took her arm. She walked so slowly, oh, so slowly. Even Weilin could crawl up the stairs faster.

When we got to her room, she wanted to lie on her bed and asked me to stack her pillows to lean on. After I got her settled, I wanted to leave, but she grabbed my arm.

"Nini, I have one more thing to ask you." She stifled a cough and held the handkerchief to her mouth. "Could you come read to me sometimes? The days get so long, and I will pay you—with books. I have some of my husband's books in English. Will you come?"

"Of course, Auntie Boxin," I agreed instantly because I was eager to get back downstairs.

"I am all right now, Nini. You may go," Auntie Boxin rasped, and her head fell back on the pillows.

I quickly went back downstairs, but I was already too late to hear the conversation and found Ma agreeing to do something with Zhao Ren.

"You won't need to go anywhere," Zhao Ren was saying. "I will bring them to you."

"But I have no textbooks," Ma said.

"That's all right. You can teach English conversation without textbooks. We need to be able to communicate."

"Of course, I can. I wanted to help but I was afraid. What if—"

"Don't worry. We will continue to keep close watch. I will send you students, one or two at a time. They will come in the evening, after dark. Gradually, I will send more. We have little money, but we can bring things you need."

Ma replied, "Don't worry about pay. I'm glad that I can do something."

They talked a little more, then Zhao Ren went to the door and was gone as quickly as he had appeared.

As soon as he left, I asked, "Ma, how do you know that he's not a spy and trying to trick us?"

Isabella spoke. "Nini, I know how you must feel. I felt the same way at first. Remember when I used to go out alone and wouldn't talk to you when I came back? I was scared and fearful then. I didn't know if I could trust anyone. After I got to know Zhao Ren and others who were resisting the Japanese, I felt I was a part of something, that I could do something."

"But why does he want Ma to teach English?"

"At some point the war will end, and when it does, the Chinese will need to be able to communicate with their new allies."

"Ma, do you trust him?" I asked.

"I don't know, Nini. All he is asking of me is to teach English. If I can be helpful, I must trust him."

In the next few days, the students started coming. One at a time, then two or three, always after dark. The younger ones, mostly college age, could speak English, but they couldn't write it. The older ones, who went to school in years past, could read but couldn't speak it. Ma used conversation at first, then created lessons for each one. I listened, but mostly I watched them. I wasn't sure what to think.

This went on for several weeks. One day someone knocked at the door. I had the hiccups but went to open it, expecting students. It was Zhao Ren! As soon as I saw him, I hiccupped.

"I have just the thing for you," he said and reached into his jacket pocket. He pulled out a small bag of something that didn't look appetizing—small, dark, shriveled knobs with a white crusty coating. "Try it," he said and held it out to me.

"No, thank you," I said, hiccupping again.

He put one in his mouth and then smiled and held the bag out to me. "They're good," he said, "and they cure hiccups."

I took one, uncertain about this shriveled thing with a white coating. The crusty surface melted into a sweet taste, and when I chewed, it was very sticky and chewy. He said it was a dried persimmon, but I wasn't sure if I liked it.

"See," he said.

"See what?"

"Your hiccups."

My hiccups had stopped.

"Here," he said, "have much."

"Not *much*," I corrected him. "*More*. Have some more."

"You see, you're a teacher," he said. "Will you be *my* teacher?"

"Yes!" I said without hesitation.

Later, when I overheard Isabella and Zhao Ren talking, he used the phrase "going over the mountains." I had a feeling that my time as his teacher would be short.

"How long will you be gone," Isabella asked tearfully.

"For a while . . . I don't know how long. Do you want to go too?" he asked Isabella.

"I want to, but I can't leave Mother now."

"I understand. I don't think it will be long, and I will see you when I return."

There was silence. I moved so I could see them, but they couldn't see me. Zhao Ren wiped tears from Isabella's cheeks, then embraced her.

"Of course," she said. "I will wait for you. But you must . . . Zhao Ren, please be careful!"

CHAPTER 17

Winter 1944

I kept track of time by winters. It was winter when we were
forced out of the water company's apartment and moved into
the mansion with Auntie Boxin. It was winter when we moved
from Auntie Boxin's to this house near the open field. This was the third
winter since the Japanese took over, and still there was no end in sight.

The mud world we had built in the summer was long gone. I missed
Zhao Ren. For some time after he left, the sweet chewiness of the dried
persimmons reminded me of him, but even they were no more. Isabella
had heard only once from him in the months since he left.

Ma's students had to stop coming, and even Auntie Boxin and
Isabella didn't come downstairs after the three of us got the whooping
cough. I had it first—just a runny nose and sneezing, then a fever that
wouldn't go away. I didn't think much of it until I started coughing.
Sometimes my coughing spells lasted so long that my face turned
purple. I couldn't catch my breath, and at the end of a spell, I'd breathe
in so fast, it made a sound like *whoop*.

By the time I started coughing, Mei-mei started sneezing. Then

Mei-mei coughed so hard she almost vomited, and Weilin got a fever. He didn't whoop like we did. He just stopped breathing altogether, and then everyone would be in a flutter until, at last, he took a breath.

According to Amah, by the time a girl was my age, twelve, she should be taking care of younger ones, not making them sick. She scolded me, "Why did you give it to the little ones? You should have stayed away from the baby." Weilin was three years old, but Amah always called him "the baby." Amah yelled at me and cooed over Weilin.

Ma had to put us in quarantine. That meant no one could come to our house and we couldn't go out. Da wasn't even allowed to enter our room. We were quarantined inside our house, and our house was quarantined from the outside world. I felt that all of China was quarantined! No one was coming in or going out.

We couldn't eat when we were coughing so hard, and we had no medicine. Ma was afraid we would die from not eating or drinking, so she tried to make us drink boiled water all the time. That was all we could take for days.

The day the quarantine ended for me, I stood by the window longing for something, for anything. I looked at the dull, gray sky, but it offered no sign of change.

I was well enough to go into the living room and be with my parents. Ma had stayed up during the night with Weilin and lay on the sofa with a damp cloth covering her eyes. Da was sitting on the arm of the sofa close to her feet. He was lighting one of the cigarettes he made from dried leaves and crushed nut hulls, while telling Ma about the Tans, a family that lived nearby.

"Mr. Tan says his wife has pains in her chest, coughing all the time, too tired to do anything. He says it's pneumonia." Da struck a match and little sparks snapped at the end of the cigarette as he sucked on it. When he blew out the smoke, he continued, "But I think it's something worse. I'm afraid she's got TB."

"What smells so awful?" Ma couldn't see Da's cigarette because of the cloth over her eyes.

Da moved to the other side of the room. Instead of sitting, he paced back and forth, still talking about the Tans.

"I told Mr. Tan when she starts spitting up blood—that's when he should get worried."

Ma sat up, leaning against the back of the sofa. "Did you say TB? I'm terrified of getting TB," she said. "I've lost so much weight it would take me out in no time."

Ma's voice didn't have much force. Her face was gray and her cheeks sunken. I couldn't tell under her padded clothes how thin she was, but I could see it in her face.

"He doesn't know if she has TB, because when he took her to the hospital, they refused her. They said Mr. Tan refused to cooperate with the Japanese, so they refused to help him." Da blew the smoke away from where Ma was. "Only those Chinese who collaborate with the Japanese can get medicine. They will pay for their crimes when the war is over!"

I wanted to cry out, *why isn't it over already?!* The war, the quarantine—all of it kept me captive. But I didn't say anything, just kept my thoughts throbbing inside my head because I knew there were no answers. I knew for certain that I couldn't stand it much longer.

All I said was, "I wish I had an orange," as if talking to myself.

Ma reacted immediately. "Nini, stop that useless thinking. You know there are no oranges. Wanting them only makes things worse."

Ma had always loved oranges, but Amah said she couldn't find any, and apples cost a hundred dollars each. Eggs or milk or meat were out of the question. But worst of all, we had no soap or coal to heat water. I never thought I would miss soap and hadn't had a bath in weeks. My hair was greasy and my back itched. I tried to scratch through my padded clothes, but it didn't help. I thought rolling on the floor might help.

This time Da was irritated with me. "Nini, quit that! You look like a dog scratching its back. Go outside if you want to act like a dog!"

Ma came to my rescue. When Da was irritable and fidgety like this, she usually tried to think of something he could do.

"I think we can abandon the quarantine now. Why don't you check on the Tans? See if there is anything we can do for them?"

That's good, I thought—*send Da outside.* He likes to be outside, and he likes to talk to people.

Then Ma turned on me. "Nini, isn't it time to resume your reading sessions with Auntie Boxin? You haven't read to her in weeks. I think you were halfway through *Oliver Twist,* weren't you?"

Now I squirmed like a dog again, this time wanting to hide under the sofa, but I knew it was useless to resist. Ma would see to it one way or the other. *Maybe Auntie Boxin will be asleep,* I thought as I plodded up the stairs. Unfortunately, Auntie Boxin was delighted to see me.

Before I got sick, I had come regularly. I dreaded these reading sessions at first. Her room was closed off to keep the warmth in, which made it smell like sour underwear. I found I could fight off the feeling of being suffocated by reading the story with exaggeration. After doing that for a while, I got caught up in the story and forgot about the smell and the stuffiness.

Isabella was glad to see me too, and when I told her Da was going to see the Tans, she said she was going out too, just for a little fresh air. For Isabella and Da, the end of the quarantine meant going outside—for me, it meant reading to Auntie Boxin in her stuffy room. *That isn't fair!*

The heavy volume of *Oliver Twist* was still on the footstool where I had left it. The footstool was where I sat when I read. I picked up the book and pushed the footstool with my foot farther away from Auntie Boxin's bed.

"Where are you going?" Auntie Boxin said, motioning me to come closer.

"I need to stay near the door—in case Ma calls," I said. But the real reason was I wanted to sneak away when Auntie Boxin fell asleep.

I flipped through the pages trying to find my place in the book, but I couldn't. Frustrated at trying to find where I left off, I decided to start at the beginning. I liked the part where Oliver is in the workhouse with the other orphans, and he approaches the workhouse master,

Mr. Bumble, with his empty bowl and asks for more gruel, "Please, sir, I want some more."

That's what I wanted to say every day, but for me there was no workhouse master to say it to.

"You've already read that part."

Auntie Boxin's eyes, which had been closed, popped open and stared right at me. Her hair was brushed back, but a few strands dropped loosely against her face.

"But I like this part. Don't you?" I knew it was rude to talk back, but I didn't care.

"It makes me sad." Her head fell back into the pillow. "When I was his age, my father died. My mother had to raise my sister and me alone. I was afraid of being an orphan." She coughed a deep, crackling cough. I backed a little further away from her bed.

"Get me a handkerchief," she croaked and motioned toward the dresser next to her bed.

I held my breath all the way to the dresser and jerked opened the top drawer, which came almost all the way out. I spied something in the back—a stack of old Chinese money from before the war. The Japanese made us use a different kind of money.

Why hadn't Auntie Boxin turned in these notes? I wondered. Now they were no good. *She could have bought food with this money!*

I let out my breath and sucked in more air in a gulp. I picked up a handkerchief with two fingers and slammed the drawer shut. Even though Amah boiled Auntie Boxin's handkerchiefs, they were dingy and stained. I barely touched it as I handed it to Auntie Boxin and held my breath, stepping back quickly.

She coughed a deep and painful cough and spit something dark into the handkerchief. She saw me staring at it.

"It's nothing," she said, folding the handkerchief in her hand and hiding it under the blanket. "Now continue reading from where you stopped the last time you were here. It's chapter eighteen."

The time seemed to go so slowly. Auntie Boxin's eyes closed

again, and I read as long as I could. When I thought she was asleep, I lowered my voice and kept talking as I eased my way toward the door.

"Where are you going, Nini?"

Startled by her voice, I tripped over the stool and the book went crashing to the floor, landing upside down, pages crushed against the spine.

"Don't harm Mr. Charles Dickens!" Auntie Boxin leaned forward from the pillow and fixed me with a glare. "Continue reading!" Auntie Boxin's head fell back as if she were exhausted, but I was the one who had been reading out loud for an hour.

I righted the stool and sat on it again, picking up the book and thumbing through the pages.

As soon as Mei-mei and Weilin were well, the quarantine ended for all of us, and Amah went into a frenzy, scrubbing everything, even without soap, from top to bottom.

Amah scolded me, "Don't you know—it's New Years?" She always chided me for not knowing Chinese things, but that morning she tried to solicit my help. "You must get ready, clean the house, sweep away bad luck, paint red characters on the door."

"But we don't have any paint," I objected.

"And make dumplings."

"We don't have any flour either."

"You are just more trouble for me," she groaned and continued scrubbing the floor.

"I have to read to Auntie Boxin." I was glad to have an excuse to get out of Amah's way and headed upstairs.

"Umph," Amah pouted.

Isabella had already cleaned up Auntie Boxin's room and thanked me for coming a little early. She said she would help Amah by going to the market. She knew the market had more things at New Years, and I knew she was just using that as an excuse to get out.

I felt trapped. I picked up the heavy book and plopped down on the footstool.

As soon as Isabella left, Auntie Boxin started coughing again. She held the handkerchief to her mouth and spit up something. She pointed with the other hand to the door and croaked, "Get my medicine."

"Where?' I asked.

She waved her hand again toward the door and mumbled something as she coughed uncontrollably.

"In the kitchen?" I asked.

She nodded as she folded the damp and darkened handkerchief. "On the . . . the . . . shelf," she choked out.

Auntie Boxin's apartment had a kitchen, but it was closed off because Amah did all the cooking downstairs. Compared to Auntie Boxin's room, the kitchen was freezing. My eyes moved quickly around the room—all sorts of jars, bottles, and containers, but I couldn't tell which was her medicine.

I began to panic. *People with TB spit up blood. What if Auntie Boxin has tuberculosis? Will we all get it? Will we all die?*

I didn't want to go back into her bedroom. I started moving jars around and opening all the cupboards, not caring what I was looking for, just delaying going back.

I opened a bottom cupboard and found only moldy old sacks. I started to close the cupboard door, but some writing on a sack caught my eye. Da had continued my Chinese lessons, so I could read many characters now. I turned one of the sacks to see the writing more clearly.

Is this really flour! There was enough for months of dumplings. I hoisted one of the sacks that felt as heavy as bricks and rushed into Auntie Boxin's room.

"Look! Look! Auntie Boxin! We have flour for New Years!" I shouted.

Auntie Boxin sat up in bed. "How dare you! That's mine! Don't touch it!" Then she began coughing uncontrollably.

"But it's New Years!" I cried. "Why can't we use it? It's just what

Amah needs to make dumplings." I had barely said the word *amah* when Auntie Boxin's face turned red.

"Do not give it to her! She stole my silver."

I was stunned. Did Auntie Boxin not understand that Amah had nothing to do with the robbery? She had been angry at Amah all this time!

"Amah didn't steal your silver, Auntie Boxin," I exclaimed. "Your servant helped the robber, not Amah! Amah tried to *stop* the robber."

Auntie Boxin had held on to this flour because she was mad at Amah and now the flour was probably too stale and moldy to eat. *What a waste!* Her misunderstanding and refusal to forgive Amah had denied us what we needed so badly.

"Not just Amah." Auntie Boxin strained to tell me something. "Once . . . my mother spilled rice in the dirt." She choked out the words. "My sister and I picked up every grain, every grain," she repeated. "Dirt and all. It was all we had to eat." She coughed again. "I kept this flour. I knew I wouldn't starve as long as I had it."

Tears stung my eyes. I didn't know about Auntie Boxin's childhood, that she had been so poor she almost starved. But still I was angry.

"Auntie Boxin, this flour is spoiled . . . and . . . and . . ." I stammered, remembering what I had found in the drawer. "And you have so much money!"

"I *had* money!" she huffed. "My husband *had* money!" She squeezed the handkerchief in her hand. "If I couldn't keep him, I could keep his money!"

I felt emboldened and said, "You must forgive Amah, Auntie Boxin. You must forgive her. It's New Years. Amah told me that New Years is the time to forgive people. Auntie Boxin, you must forgive Amah and give her this flour for New Year's."

She shook her fist with the bloody handkerchief at me, "Take it!" She cried in her raspy voice, "Take it to Amah!"

Amah cried when I brought her the sacks of flour. I couldn't tell if she was crying out of joy for the flour or sorrow because it was spoiled. When she opened the sack, the flour smelled rancid and moldy. I could see little wormy bugs wiggling around in it. Amah pinched one with her fingers and shook her head.

Amah got to work. I helped her sift the flour with a tightly woven basket. She cut up wild onions from the field and garlic she had grown and dried. She mixed the onions and garlic with a few vegetables for the filling. She made a dough with the flour and rolled it and cut it into circles. She put a spoonful of the vegetable filling onto each circle and then folded it over and pinched the edges. First, she boiled them, then fried them.

"That will kill any bugs," she said, "and besides, it won't hurt us if we do eat them."

Isabella came home from the market with a few things for Amah, and red paper, banners, and a lantern. I helped her hang the lantern. She showed Mei-mei how to make Chinese paper cuts with the red paper, and they hung them on the windows. Da had taught me how to write the characters for happiness, long life, and prosperity—*Fu Lu Shou*. I wrote them on the banners and hung them around the room.

That night we celebrated the New Year with *jiaozi*, dumplings that signified a good wish for our family. The garlic and onions hid the taste of the spoiled flour, at least to our eager tongues. We took the dumplings to Auntie Boxin and thanked her for the gift. When Amah brought her the bowl of *jiaozi*, I saw tears in Auntie Boxin's eyes. We wished her health and a good year.

Ma, Da, Mei-mei, Weilin, Isabella and I gathered round the table with anticipation. It was the Year of the Monkey, and Mei-mei put the brass monkey in the center of the table, decorated with her Chinese paper cuts. Amah had said anyone born in the Year of the Monkey was intelligent, well-liked, and successful in every way. Mei-mei was grinning, but she was not born in the Year of the Monkey—I was!

"Nini, did you know the brass monkey is the Monkey King?" Da asked. "Your mother gave him to me after my journey to the West, to New York. You see, the Monkey King made a Journey to the West, too. See his boots? He can walk on clouds. And did he cause havoc! In many ways he's like you, Nini. He's curious and restless and prone to outbursts, but in the long run, he served his master and brought him safely to India."

I turned thirteen that night even though my birthday wasn't until December.

We played cards and laughed and stayed up late. The next morning, I wrote calligraphy with a brush and put the banner on the door: happiness, long life, and prosperity, and I added another one—*Ping An*, peace.

I wanted this to be the last winter that we were trapped inside, the last winter that China was quarantined. I wished things would return to normal, but I wanted, most of all, to see Chiyoko again.

CHAPTER 18

Spring 1944

"Carry this stick," Amah said to Mei-mei, handing her a cane she had cut last summer from the reeds in the field. Amah held a longer and stronger stick and carried some bags she had made from the flour sacks. "Let's go now."

Amah was taking us to find wild greens that grew along the creek. I went ahead of them out the gate carrying nothing, glad to be going outside, even if we were *foraging*, as Ma called it.

The air was nippy, and I pulled the sleeves of Ma's old sweater down over my hands for warmth. I had outgrown my own sweaters. All I had now were Ma's old baggy things. This sweater was made of blue-gray Scottish wool, and at one time Ma thought it was so smart looking, but by the time it came to me, it was worn and faded and had patches on the sleeves.

I drank in the cool freshness of the early March morning. I was glad to be outside before the winds blew in the awful yellow dust that came every spring. I was ready for a break, and I set out in front of Amah and Mei-mei, heading straight for the open field.

The field looked nothing like it had in the summer. The tall grasses where we had hidden from the boys were now beaten down by the winter rains. There were no places to hide, no secret paths, no jeweled grasshoppers to find. Broken stubble stuck up in places from the matted grass, and the hard tips poked at my feet and snagged my padded pants.

"Not that way," called Amah.

I turned and saw Amah and Mei-mei headed toward a marshy area down near the creek on the far side of the field. In the summer, the creek was dry, but in the spring, it flowed, filling the marshes around it with water. Amah said the watercress in the creek and the shoots in the marsh were good to eat.

When I caught up with them, Amah handed me a bag.

"Look here," she said, bending and pulling up a clump of matted grasses, wet and beaten down. Underneath the clump were tiny green shoots of wild millet.

Amah tried to instruct us. "You see. Winter comes, winter goes, and new life starts. We can eat these. Pick it this way." Amah pinched the little green shoots and put them in her bag.

Mei-mei stood there, her bag hanging limply from one hand and her other hand holding her cane as she stared at her wet feet, the cloth shoes Amah had made, squishing in the mud. She reached out for a tall stem.

"No, no, not that one," Amah corrected. Amah knew which shoots we could eat and which ones we couldn't.

I was wearing Ma's old flats with socks. I didn't want to get wet and have to walk back across the stubbly field with frozen feet, so I wandered off a little, avoiding the marshy area, but staying close to where the ground was drier. I could still hear Amah telling Mei-mei about her childhood in the countryside, about how she used to pick greens with her mother, how she knew where to look—stories I had heard before and didn't want to hear again, at least not on this day, my first day in the open fields.

I hadn't seen a day like this in so long. There were only a few clouds in the blue sky. I wasn't looking at my feet anymore. I was looking at the sky. I gazed out in the distance. *When will the American planes come?* I wondered if the planes would fly over this field. If they did, I might be the first to see them.

I heard a rustling on the ground, and something slithered across my foot. I jumped. In a move so fast I could hardly see what happened, a black snake lunged forward and swallowed something.

"Amah!" I shouted. "Come quickly! A snake!"

"What? A snake?" Amah held her stick in the air and ran toward me. She moved faster than I had ever seen her, and she reached me in no time. In a flash, with her raised stick, she whacked the snake hard.

To my amazement, a frog popped out of the snake's mouth and did a little hop, as if nothing out of the ordinary had happened. The snake lunged forward and swallowed the frog again.

"Did you see that?"

Mei-mei sloshed over to us, her wet feet making her move more slowly. "I want to see it!" she cried as she reached us. "What happened?"

"A snake swallowed a frog," I said excitedly. "And when Amah hit it, the frog hopped out of its mouth."

"I want to see it. Where's the frog?" she asked.

"The snake swallowed it again."

"Do it again, Amah. Do it again!" Mei-mei pleaded.

Amah already had the stick raised and brought it down on the snake's head. Whop—out popped the frog again. This time the frog seemed a bit more dazed, but still it took a little hop.

Before Mei-mei could request it, the snake swallowed the frog a third time!

The snake must be as hungry as everyone else and determined to die full, I thought.

Amah wanted to finish the job this time, so she whacked the snake harder. The frog popped out and hopped away while she kept hitting the snake again and again. Finally, Amah picked him up by the end. The long, thin, black snake hung from her hand, lifeless.

"Well," she said, "He won't eat the frog, but we will eat him. Open your bag, Nini."

I hesitantly opened the bag, and she dropped the snake in. I held the top of the bag tightly. Amah continued picking greens. By the time Amah said we had enough, my hands and feet were cold. The sky had turned gray, and clouds were moving in as we trudged back across the stubbled field.

"Do you think the planes will come from that direction?" I asked, looking off to the east over the field. I knew the Pacific Ocean was not far. I wasn't speaking to anyone in particular, just talking out loud to keep my mind off my feet.

Amah's attention was on the ground, not on the sky.

"Why talk about planes? Useless thinking. War is like winter. It comes, it goes, and we go on. I don't see planes. You are looking far away. Look here. Think about the snake. Think about the frog."

Mei-mei hadn't been paying attention to either of us. She was plodding along behind us, but when she heard Amah, she said, "Poor little frog."

"Don't worry about the frog," Amah admonished.

"But . . ." Mei-mei slowed.

"You don't need to worry about the frog," Amah said, trudging ahead. "The frog is like China. The snake swallows him, just like Japan swallows China, but look, the frog lives and the snake's dead. Just you wait. You'll see."

I was walking next to Amah, still holding the snake in the bag. It was hard for me to be like Amah. It was natural for her to look for frogs and snakes, but I liked to think about things I didn't have. Ma once scolded me for wanting oranges because it was useless to think we could have them. But thinking about oranges and looking for airplanes gave me hope that things would change.

"When we get home, I'll show you something you won't forget," Amah said to me. I could tell she was happy with the results of our foraging. "Would you like to see how my mother taught me to eat a snake?"

CHAPTER 19

Summer 1945

I was writing a letter to Chiyoko when Amah asked me to go with her to the market to get the food we bought with Auntie Boxin's rations. We were relying almost completely on them now.

Ma had resumed teaching, and I helped her with the lessons. "I can't go. I have to prepare my lesson for Ma," I said. I didn't tell her I was writing to Chiyoko. She would accuse me of wasting my time.

Instead of scolding me, Amah grabbed Mei-mei's hand and dragged her along, even though Mei-mei complained she didn't feel like going.

As soon as they were gone, I became restless, wishing I had gone to the market instead of Mei-mei. My restlessness made me want to see Chiyoko even more. It had been over three years since we had parted in the garden. I had written a stack of letters to her, but there was no way to get them to the secret hiding place. And what was worse, I didn't know if she had left any messages for me.

Two of Ma's students came for an English lesson. I tried to talk to them, but Ma told me she didn't need me that day. She knew I had used this as an excuse not to go with Amah, and she was punishing me. I tried to write but couldn't concentrate and kept getting up to look out the window. Ma's students left before Amah and Mei-mei returned. I was still sulking and didn't pay any attention when Mei-mei went straight to her room.

"Is Mei-mei all right?" Ma asked Amah.

"Just hot and tired," said Amah. "We waited long time in sun."

"It's not like her to go to bed. I'll check on her."

I followed behind Ma, feeling bad that I hadn't gone. Mei-mei had fallen across the bed with her clothes on, even her shoes. Ma put her hand on Mei-mei's forehead. Her hair was sticking to her brow.

"Oh, my," exclaimed Ma. "Nini, get me a damp cloth."

By the time I got back, Ma had taken off Mei-mei's shoes and loosened her clothes. Mei-mei's eyes were closed. Ma wiped her face with the damp cloth, and then laid it across her forehead. Mei-mei blinked and looked at Ma, but she didn't say anything.

"Is she all right?" I asked.

"I don't know for sure, but you should stay away, just in case."

Ma pressed her fingers against Mei-mei's wrist to check her pulse. Mei-mei began to wet the bed.

"Tell Amah to come quickly!"

I ran to get Amah, but by the time she arrived, a watery, dark, yellowish mess oozed across the bed. Mei-mei lay right in the middle of it.

"Help me get the sheets off," Ma ordered Amah. "Don't let any of it get on you. Nini, stay out."

I stood at the door. Ma showed more strength than she had in months. She lifted Mei-mei, while Amah removed the sheet from the bed and folded it with the mess on the inside.

"Wash it in boiling water, then hang it in the sun. This is very important."

Amah left with the sheets, and Ma took off Mei-mei's clothes and put a loose gown on her.

"I can take her clothes to Amah, if you want me to," I said, trying to help from the doorway.

"Don't touch anything!"

Mei-mei was limp as a rag doll. Her skin was damp, her hair stringy, her eyes open but unfocused, dreamlike. She mumbled things that didn't make any sense.

"I don't understand it," Ma said. "A few minutes ago, her face was flushed, and she was hot all over. Now her limbs are chilled, hands cold as ice."

Without even looking up, Ma said, "Nini, get a blanket from my room, not the wool one—it's too itchy."

I ran to Ma's room and came back as quickly as I could. I handed a cotton padded blanket to Ma, barely going past the door.

"Tell Amah to come."

I found Amah outside gathering anything she could to light a fire. Amah had a pile of reeds from the field, and she combined them with sticks for fueling the fire.

"How does she expect me to clean these things with no soap!" she muttered.

"Come, quick!" I said.

When we got to the room, Ma had wrapped the cotton blanket around Mei-mei's limp, chilled body and had placed Mei-mei on the bed.

"Take these clothes and wash them with the sheets. Be careful and use very hot water."

Then Ma went to the bathroom, scrubbed her hands, and called, "Nini, you do the same. Wash your hands, all the way up to your elbows."

I tried to wash, but we only had a stone, which felt like a piece of concrete to wash with. It hurt as I rubbed the rough surface across my hands and arms. By the time I finished, Da had come home, and I overheard Ma talking to him in the living room.

"I think I know what this is," Ma said. "I saw it as a child. In the summers, usually in children, but I . . . I haven't seen typhoid in years. I don't know where she got it. This could be very serious."

Da took a long, deep breath and let out a sigh of frustration and anger. "Everyone is forced to live in these unhealthy conditions. I've heard there are many outbreaks of cholera and typhoid."

"I thought we'd be safe since we're so isolated."

"Mei-mei could have gotten it anywhere, from the water, the marsh, the lousy food, anything." Da was always angry at the conditions we lived in and blamed it on the Japanese and their Chinese collaborators.

"We've got to get help," Ma said anxiously.

"All the doctors I know have left, and the hospitals won't take us. We'll have to take care of her ourselves."

"When I was a child, we had an outbreak of typhoid, and my brother was sick. I remember the country doctor saying that milk and limewater were the only things to give him, that anything else was injurious."

"We can't get those things. Milk costs over a hundred dollars a glass, if you can even find it." Da added, "And there are no limes."

"No, not limes. *Limewater* is not from limes. It's alkaline water."

"Ah, yes, I remember what it is. Sun used it sometimes."

Ma's face brightened. "Sun! He will help us. He can find it, but how can we find him?"

"I know where he is," Da said. "He's working for Madame Lu, the mayor's sister. But the mayor is a traitor! We can't hope for any help from her. I'll have to find it myself."

"There's no way you can go! Mr. Yasemoto has blackened your name in the city, and too many people would recognize you. What about me? I could disguise myself. I could cover my head with a black shawl. I'd look like a Chinese grandmother, and no one would recognize me. I could go at night."

"You'd never pass as Chinese. Besides you'd have to find your way alone, and it's too dangerous to go at night."

While they were talking, I wandered back outside to find Amah, who was stoking the fire with dried reeds to get the pot boiling. She had added Mei-mei's clothes to the sheets in the pot. The smoke caused my eyes to water and my throat to choke up. I moved away from the smoke and when my throat cleared, I asked Amah if she knew how to reach Sun.

"Sun! You ask about Sun. He's no help to us," she grunted.

Amah used to be fond of Sun, but now she was disgusted with him, thinking him a traitor for working for Madame Lu.

"How could Sun work for someone like that? Just so he can eat. I won't have anything to do with Sun anymore."

I pushed on. "Where does Madame Lu live?" Not wanting to make her suspicious, I added, "Auntie Boxin was asking."

"Well, Auntie Boxin should know," she replied, not looking up as she cautiously pushed the sheets and clothes in the hot water with her stick. "Auntie Boxin lived on the same street. You know, that big house on the opposite corner, the one with the brick wall around it."

I passed that way every day when I went to the Chinese school, but I wasn't exactly sure which one she meant—nearly all the houses had brick walls around them.

Amah kept on. "But I don't know why Auntie Boxin wants to know. She hasn't even been outside the house. She doesn't know what has happened. People are hungry and will rob her of everything."

"Well, if you *had* to, which way would you go?"

"If I had to, I'd go through the marsh. On the other side of the marsh, there's a longer way that avoids the barracks. But I wouldn't do it, even if Tai-tai demanded!"

I went back into the house and found Ma and Da still talking about what to do. I stood in the doorway for a moment, not knowing what to say. I wanted to go myself. In the past I would have just gone, without permission, maybe without telling anyone. But that was not possible now, and I knew my parents would never let me go, even if I knew Amah's way. Then I heard Ma sigh.

"Well, we have to do something," she said. "We have to find Sun."

There from the doorway, without even going into the room, I blurted, "I will go. I can find Sun. I know the way, and no one will suspect me. I can get there faster than anyone."

Ma and Da stared at me in disbelief. Ma protested and cried, remembering what had happened the time I went to see Chiyoko. Da was silent at first, but when Ma finished, he spoke calmly.

"Nini, I understand your spirit. Let's talk about the danger. People from the countryside have poured into the city looking for food. They are hungry and desperate." Da had already explained that food went first to the Japanese and then to those who collaborated with them. "The peasants have no place in the city to live. Many of them have settled in the old army barracks where your school used to be. It's dangerous to go that way. They will rob anyone."

"Amah has told me a way to go through the marsh and avoid the barracks. She says it takes longer, but if I follow Amah's way, I know I can do it."

"I don't know Amah's way, but I will check with her and see if it is better."

We kept talking, until Ma reluctantly gave in. When the matter was settled, Da said, "I will write a letter to Sun, explaining everything. Now get some sleep."

CHAPTER 20

*A*ll night I lay in the bed thinking about the way I would go. I wasn't as sure of Amah's way as I wanted to be. I knew how to cross the field and go to the marsh, but I didn't know how to get through the marsh or where I would come out on the other side.

What if I got lost? What if I couldn't find Sun? My biggest fear was that Sun would refuse to see me. Surely, he would be glad to see me, but what if he had changed or if Madame Lu wouldn't let him help us? Every time these doubts arose, I thought, *I have to find him! Mei-mei might not live if I don't.*

The next morning, Amah woke me early and prepared food for me to take.

"Don't drink any water from the stream," she warned. "It will make you sick." She found one of Ma's jars and filled it with boiled water.

Ma had been up in the night with Mei-mei and her eyes were dark and puffy. Da had talked to Amah and agreed that her way was safer and gave me his letter to Sun, which I put in my knapsack.

Heading for the front door, I spotted the Monkey King on the table. I remembered all the times Mei-mei had played with him, hiding Da's cigarettes or decorating for New Years. I choked back tears, then picked him up and put him in my knapsack.

Ma and Amah said goodbye at the door, giving me last minute instructions and begging me to be careful. Da walked with me to the gate, giving his advice and telling me to return by nightfall.

The sky was beginning to lighten. Pale pink and coral showed on the horizon. The grasses in the field seemed to waken in the glow of the early morning light. It reminded me of the mornings when Chiyoko and I used to meet for school. Our walks to school and back were our best times together. I wanted desperately to know if she had left a message for me.

The secret garden was in the direction that Amah told me to go, but I wasn't familiar with Amah's way. It went through the Chinese section that she knew well but I didn't. I might get lost trying to find the garden. I had to keep my focus on my task -- to find Sun and get back home before dark. It seemed to me that I could get there faster if I went the way I knew. I turned and headed toward the barracks.

I walked quickly, and soon I became aware of my empty stomach. It made me feel less hungry to think about my favorite meals Sun used to cook. One time when Chiyoko stayed with me, Sun made fried chicken and served it with mashed potatoes, peas, carrots and homemade applesauce. It was an American-style dinner that Ma liked, but Ma thought Mei-mei was too little to eat adult food, so she smashed the peas and carrots into the potatoes for her. Mei-mei moved the mashed food around on her plate. When Ma wasn't looking, she went to the kitchen and put it in the garbage and ate Sun's *tsin-tsai* with garlic and bamboo shoots.

Oh, how Chiyoko and I had laughed at her. Mei-mei was always doing funny things. I wanted her to be well and make me laugh again. If only she could smell Sun's cooking again—that would make her feel better.

Suddenly a foul smell like human waste and rotten garbage turned my stomach. The morning was still only light enough that I could make out mounds of garbage of nameless things. A rat scurried over a pile. A scrawny dog gnawed on the bones of a dead animal. A girl about Mei-mei's size stood on the edge of one pile and squatted to pee. A little boy near her, holding a bag in his hands, stared at me with tired eyes.

Da was right. I hardly recognized the old barracks where I had gone to the Chinese school. Windows were broken out completely and doors torn off the buildings. The doors were used as lean-tos against the walls. What I thought were lumps of garbage at first were people lying against the walls or using removed doors for shelter. Some dark shapes, like shadows wrapped in pitiful rags, moved around the heaps.

An old man leaned against an iron lamppost. His eyes were following me. I was confused for a moment when I thought he nodded at me. Then something hit me from behind, and two arms reached around me.

I turned my head and stared into the smudged face of a boy slightly smaller than me. His arms were short and bony and couldn't reach all the way around me, so he grabbed the straps of my knapsack and yanked. I pulled my arms tight together. *He's not taking my knapsack!* It had everything—food for the day, water to drink, a letter for Sun.

In a flash, I remembered that Chiyoko's dragonfly was still in the knapsack. *I cannot lose it!* I thought of the picture of St. Patrick that Tooner gave me—*Protect me now,* I prayed. I jerked hard and pulled away from the boy.

Out of the corner of my eye, I saw the old man moving toward me. Suddenly a dog leaped from a mound of trash and landed on a makeshift shelter as he bounded for us, causing the iron lamppost to tilt.

"Watch out!" I yelled, but it was too late.

The lean-to collapsed and the heavy lamppost fell, hitting the old man and pinning him to the ground.

The boy cried out, "Grandpa!" He ran and knelt over the old man, and the dog ran to the boy and licked his face.

I could have run away then, but something pulled me back.

The old man groaned pitifully. The boy spoke to him. He pushed the dog away and tried to move the post, lifting and grunting. His hands were too small and his arms too weak. I knew he would never be able to lift it alone. The boy looked at me with distressed and pleading eyes. I joined him and together we dragged the heavy lamppost off the old man and placed it to the side.

The old man moved slightly, then groaned again. The boy knelt beside him, and the old man asked for water. I knelt and fumbled in my knapsack and found the jar that Amah had given me. The old man could not sit up, so I stuck my fingers in the water and rubbed some on the old man's lips. He licked it off, and I did it again. After a few minutes, the man seemed to gain strength, and the boy helped him sit up and drink from my jar. When he had enough, he nodded to me. I took it as his way of saying thanks. It was quite different from his nod a few minutes before, telling the boy to jump on me.

The boy was helping the old man when I stood and started to put the jar back in my knapsack. I saw the boy look at the jar. That was all the water I had, but I handed the jar to the boy and hoisted the knapsack on my shoulders. I started walking away, heading the way I had come. The boy jumped up and motioned me to follow him.

I hesitated, but he motioned again. I followed him around the mounds of garbage. More people were moving around, and their dark eyes stared at me.

The boy led me through the barracks to the street on the other side. I was relieved when I recognized where I was. This was the way I used to walk to Auntie Boxin's house when I went to the Chinese school. I smiled to thank him. He didn't smile back, but he gestured with his hand toward the street, his eyes pleading with me to go.

I walked straight ahead, turning back only once and saw the boy still watching out for me until I was safely away from the barracks. I turned the corner and could see him no more.

CHAPTER 21

As soon as I was out of sight of the boy, I dropped my knapsack and reached for the red box. I took out the dragonfly and latched the chain around my neck. Tucking the pendant under my shirt, I put my hand over it, remembering Chiyoko's words. *"If a dragonfly lands on you, it's good luck."* I didn't want to risk losing it, and, besides, I needed all the luck I could get.

It was daylight now, and I had no trouble finding my way, but I hadn't been in this area since the foreigners had been forced out. The houses looked deserted, gates left open, and pieces of furniture were strewn in the courtyards as if they were bodies dragged out and left to rot.

It seemed strange to me that so many foreigners had lived here. That had never seemed strange before. I had just accepted the way it was. It didn't seem right that foreigners had made this part of China their home, but now they were gone, and I felt sad.

Where had they been taken after I saw them getting on those buses at the Empire Hotel? Was Tooner still whistling? Did Paul Thompson find another short-wave radio? Had Tommy grown tall like his dad? I wondered if Mrs. Powell was still wearing her fur coat. And Dr. Meyer. Did he regret that he had not gone back to Holland?

I moved quickly without thinking where to go as if my feet knew the way on their own. When I passed the street where the banner had hung and the drunken soldiers celebrated Singapore's defeat, I knew I was not far from Auntie Boxin's. Still the memory of that military music and loud shouts and singing made me clench my hands until I realized there were no roadblocks or guards. Without the foreigners, there was no need to stop anyone or to check their registration or turn people back because of their armbands.

It was still early when I approached Auntie's Boxin's. Even if it took me a while to find the house where Sun was living, he would be busy preparing breakfast for Madame Lu and he might not have time for me. If I knocked on his door, he might not answer.

I wonder if Chiyoko has left me a message? Thinking I had time to go to the secret garden and still get to Sun's in time, I turned toward the former French district.

When I reached the French park, I felt disoriented. The rose bushes and fruit trees that had lined the walkway were cut down or badly damaged. The sandbox where Mei-mei used to play with the other foreign children was destroyed and the sand scattered.

The row of shops fared no better. I was stunned to find the green and white awnings ripped down, lying in charred shreds. The bakery was burned. The shop windows were broken, and trash lay across the front. The iron gates of the French ambassador's residence were barred with a heavy chain.

The Rue de France was almost deserted. Only a few people were about, some pushing carts or carrying loads, but there was no sign of the former life I had known there. No rickshaws or pedicabs, no minitruck drivers honking and yelling at a bicycle or cart driver to get out of the way. And no policeman with his whistle and white-gloved hand to direct the noisy traffic. But also, there were no Japanese guards! The four soldiers with rifles and bayonets were no longer posted at the intersection. I crossed without needing the sweet potato man to hide behind.

I was relieved to see that St. George's Cathedral was still standing as before. The three crosses, three domes, and three arches were just the same, but it looked cold and empty. I quickly slipped down the path through the cemetery.

The oleander bushes were overgrown, and I had to push them back to find the hole in the wall. Despite more bricks having fallen on the ground, the hole seemed narrower than I remembered. Afraid that I couldn't get through, I dropped to my knees and looked through the gap to the garden. I couldn't see past the bushes on the other side. I took off my knapsack, and turning sideways as I had before, I squeezed through and reached back for my bag.

The garden felt completely abandoned. The broken glass on the top of the walls seemed useless because places in the wall had tumbled down. The statue on the fountain had fallen over and was hanging upside down in twisted vines. Weeds had taken over the rest of the place.

It made me sad, but I didn't waste time and looked for the pile of bricks that marked the spot.

I pulled the brick sticking out from the wall and let it drop it to the ground. Looking in, I could see something in the hollow space. My heart leapt. My fingers reached for a folded piece of paper.

The paper was dingy and the writing faded. In some places I could barely make out what it said.

Nini,

I am afraid you will never see this. I heard the foreigners were taken away. I'm afraid your mother or your whole family is gone.

After father was forced------ mother has been ill ------don't try to come to the clinic. ----- dangerous. I will ----

The last part was blurred, but I had learned the most important thing—when she wrote this note, Chiyoko was still living at the clinic with her mother.

But she thinks I have been taken away with the other foreigners! I must leave something for her.

I wished I had brought the letters that I had written to her, but they would never fit in the hole. I was afraid that even if I left a message, she no longer came to look.

So much time had passed since she wrote this message that she might have moved. I wanted to see her so desperately. I wanted to knock on the clinic door, but what if she didn't live there anymore? What if someone there arrested me? If I got caught, I would never find Sun and my family would never find me!

I've come this far. I have to see her.

I put Chiyoko's note in my knapsack, and without placing the brick back in the hole, I left the garden through the gate.

The sky had lightened as I moved from the alley to the street. The shops were closed. Bodies that had been sleeping against walls moved like dark shadows. The smell of urine stung my nostrils. I held on to my knapsack tighter with each step.

I was relieved when I saw the building with the sign, *Closed in the name of the Emperor of Japan.* The red paint on the sign was faded and peeling. I passed the clinic doors and went around to the unmarked door in the back.

My hand froze as I started to knock. What if Chiyoko's family had been forced to move and someone else opened the door? I would be standing face to face with a stranger. I hesitated. Then knowing I had no other way to see Chiyoko, I knocked.

My heart pounded. When no one answered, I stepped away, then knocked even louder.

After a minute or so, the door opened slightly. My heart leapt to my throat, and I couldn't speak.

The silence seemed to last forever. The person on the other side of the door spoke first. It was a man speaking Chinese.

"The clinic has been closed a long time. Not taking any patients. Don't come here anymore," he said and shut the door.

I spoke up quickly. "Please. I'm not coming for the clinic. I'm looking for Chiyoko." The door stayed closed, but I didn't hear the clank of the latch.

The man's voice came through the door. "Chiyoko? How do you know Chiyoko?"

"I'm Nini. I'm her school friend."

"Is anyone with you?"

"No."

The door opened. The man was dressed in a robe, his hair uncombed.

"Nini! Of course I remember you." His voice softened. "But we thought . . . we thought you had been taken away."

The door opened wide.

"Come inside quickly. I'm so sorry. Please forgive me. We have to be careful. How in the world have you survived? Come upstairs. Chiyoko will be so glad to see you!" Dr. Mori changed from Chinese to English somewhere in the middle of his greeting.

As we walked up the stairs, Dr. Mori continued. "I apologize for my English. I have no opportunities to use it now. No English-speaking people come to the hospital. I am usually there, but I'm so glad I am home today. Chiyoko will be so happy. So will my wife—she needs some cheering up."

Dr. Mori opened the door to the apartment upstairs and told me to go in first. Mrs. Mori lay on the sofa under the window. The window was covered with black cloth, the only light coming from a small lamp on the table beside her.

Chiyoko was sitting beside her. The darkness around her eyes was no match for the brightness in her face when she saw me. I was overjoyed. We laughed at the surprise of seeing each other.

"You're taller," I said.

"So are you," she laughed. My hair was in long braids, hers tied in back.

Mrs. Mori welcomed me. Her voice was hoarse, and she apologized for not getting up.

Dr. Mori began to explain their situation.

"As you can see, the officers closed our clinic and threatened to send Chiyoko and her mother to Japan. I convinced them to let them stay since her mother is Chinese and this is her home. I have been an outcast ever since we married. At first, I was forbidden to work at the hospital, but my help is desperately needed. There are so few Japanese doctors here. So, I agreed to work at the hospital for long periods. Chiyoko has taken care of her mother. But now—"

"I couldn't have made it without Chiyoko," her mother said. She coughed and spit into a handkerchief. I recognized that cough.

Her father continued, "I have been able to get medicine and food for both of them from the hospital. Otherwise, we couldn't have made it."

Her mother interrupted. "It's all right. I am sure she understands, but she has come for a reason. Would you like some tea?"

Before I could say anything, Chiyoko grabbed my hand. "Yes, let's make some tea. Come with me."

As soon as we were in the kitchen, Chiyoko lit the stove, and I said, "I just saw your message. I had to come! You see—"

"My message! I left that message nearly three years ago. There was no other way to contact you. Hearing nothing, I assumed you were taken away with the foreigners."

"No, no. I saw them being forced on the buses. I told Da about it and we moved that night. We have kept Ma hidden inside the house all this time. Isabella and Auntie Boxin live upstairs. But I'm worried. Auntie Boxin . . . she coughs like your mother."

"Oh, Nini, I fear that Mother will die."

"Don't think that way. She must hold on."

"But I don't think she can make it much longer. She only gets weaker and coughs so much."

As she was preparing the tea, I took my necklace off. "Chiyoko, your dragonfly has helped me."

Chiyoko stared at the bulging eyes and blue-green wings.

"You must wear it now. It will remind you that change is coming. It's good luck to wear the dragonfly."

I put the necklace around her neck, and she held it with her hand, tears in her eyes.

"Thank you, Nini. I need this so much."

The water was boiling now. "I'm sorry, but this is all we have." She was holding a tin of barley tea. "Is this all right?"

"Of course, it is. We haven't had tea of any sort for a long time."

When she had a pot of tea ready, she carried a tray with four cups to the other room.

Dr. Mori was standing by the sofa where Chiyoko's mother lay. He had set two chairs and a small table nearby and motioned me to sit there. Chiyoko poured tea and the four of us talked. I told them everything that had happened to us and then about Mei-mei and why I had come. Dr. Mori said medicine was in short supply, but that he would send something with me that would help her rest. Then he told me the news.

"The people at the hospital are talking of nothing else. The Americans are bombing Tokyo. The destruction, fires are everywhere."

"What does it mean?" I asked, staring at Dr. Mori.

"No one knows for sure, but the end must be near."

"Do you mean the war is over?"

"No," he said. "Not yet. At least not in China. Anything can still happen."

Chiyoko's mother was agitated. "Why has it taken so long?"

"It may take longer," Dr. Mori cautioned. "We must be careful."

Chiyoko was nearly in tears. "But it can't take longer. It can't! Something has to change." She reached her hand to the necklace.

We talked about the state of the war a bit longer until I realized the time. "I must go! I have to find Sun and get home tonight."

Chiyoko dashed into the kitchen and came back with a small packet of barley tea. "Here, take this. Tell Mei-mei as soon as things change, we will come see her."

Dr. Mori gave me a small bottle of medicine and said, "Tell Mei-mei this may help her sleep. But she must be strong and we will come to see her, as soon as the war ends."

My voice choked as I said goodbye. "Thank you. You have given me more than tea and medicine. You have given me hope."

CHAPTER 22

I was tired by the time I reached Auntie Boxin's. The house looked different than it had the night when we first arrived in the rickshaws. I had been intimidated in the dark with Auntie Boxin at the top of the steps, but now it seemed dilapidated; the paint was peeling, and an upstairs shutter had fallen off.

How strange it seemed that only Auntie Boxin and Isabella had lived in this huge house; such a waste. When Auntie Boxin moved out, she hadn't sold it, so I assumed it must be abandoned.

I was surprised when I heard noises coming from inside—the sound of voices, the clinking of dishes. *Does Auntie Boxin know someone is living in her house? I should find out who and tell her.*

I slipped around to the back, following the servants' entrance, creeping along the shrubs below the windows. I could see into the kitchen. Men were sitting around a table. They were wearing loose pants and white undershirts in the heat. The window was open, and a fan was blowing. One of the men left the room. The others were arguing. I couldn't make out what they were saying.

I moved closer, pushing a branch away from my face so I could see more clearly, when I heard a man's voice behind me say in Japanese, "Hey! What are you doing?"

I dropped the branch and gasped. Looking down so he wouldn't see my face, I noticed he wore only slippers. He must have come outside hastily.

"You little runt! What are you doing here?" His voice was gruff.

I had to use all my wits. I dropped to my knees and bowed completely to the ground. I began begging him in Chinese not to hurt me.

"I will teach you not to spy!"

He moved toward me, as if to kick me, but his slipper fell off and he stopped. He grabbed my hair by the braids and yanked my head back. Then he pulled on the knapsack strap and jerked me up. One strap of the knapsack came off my shoulder. He grabbed at it with one hand and his other hand flew up as if to strike me.

Just then a shout came from inside. It sounded like someone calling him. He hesitated, dropped his arm and said something in disgust, put his slipper back on, and turned toward the door, calling to the others. His slippers flip-flopped up the back steps and into the house.

I jerked my knapsack back on my shoulders and ran out the servants' entrance and down the street, my heart pounding. I was not sure where to go. Several houses had brick walls, but Amah had said it was the one on the corner opposite Auntie Boxin's. I ran to the one on the corner and banged desperately on the gate. The wood gate was too high to see over and had no latticework.

I looked back over my shoulder. No one was coming. I beat on the gate again. I heard a faint female voice ask from the other side.

"What is your business?"

"Please, I am looking for Sun Baosan," I pleaded.

"Wait," she said, and I heard her footsteps swishing away. Tall sycamores lined the street, but the branches of the sycamore trees were high, so there was no place to hide. *If Sun doesn't work here, wouldn't she have told me to go away? What if she went to get the owner and he's Japanese?*

I heard heavier footsteps and the sound of metal clanking. The gate opened.

"Why, Nini! Look at you! How you have grown!"

I probably looked taller to him because my sleeves were too short, but Sun looked glorious to me. Before, he had looked like a boy, but now he was a man, plumper too, with more hair. He was dressed in a white mandarin-style chef jacket with a high collar and tie buttons down the front.

He exclaimed, "Your braids are so long!"

I glanced over my shoulder once more.

"Come inside," he said.

I entered and he shut the gate and bolted it.

"Sit here," he said, gesturing to a bench in the courtyard. Then he sat next to me. "It has been so long. How is your father?"

"Da? He's all right. Well, restless most of the time. He can't stay still."

"What about your mother?"

"She is all right too, but very tired and—"

"How old is your little brother now? He must be, what? Three? four?"

"Four . . . but Sun," I stammered.

"And your sister, quite the little tiger as always, I bet!"

"Mei-mei—" My voice cracked, and I started to choke. Sun moved closer to me, and my head fell onto his chest. "Oh, Sun!" I cried.

"There, there," he said, patting my back. Then he leaned over and whispered in my ear, "Don't say anything else. Follow me." He got up and said in a voice louder than necessary for just me to hear. "There is nothing wrong with you that a little tea won't help. Come inside."

I followed him around to the back of the house to a doorway partially hidden by a lattice frame covered in vines.

Inside, we stepped down to a dark hall. He opened another door, and we entered a room that felt like it was underground except for small windows high on the other side. Even in the dim light, I could tell it was neat and comfortable. The dirt floor was covered by a mat made of rushes. There was a long brick bench with bedding rolled up, making a place to sit. A coal stove was lit, and he motioned me to sit.

"Youmei, bring some tea," Sun called out in Chinese. "We have a guest."

A young woman came in, wearing a long, gray jacket over black pants, similar to the ones that Amah wore. She began moving about the stove, lifting the big kettle already full and poured hot water into a teapot. A toddler with short black hair, big red cheeks, and steady eyes peered at me from behind the door.

The young woman, I assumed to be his wife, poured the tea into two cups. Sun whispered something to her, and she left the room. The toddler started to follow her, but she nudged him back with gentle words. The little one crouched behind Sun's chair and peeked around to look at me.

"Now," he said more solemnly. "Tell me why you came on this dangerous journey."

"I came because we must have milk and lime water. Can you help us?" I began, but then started fumbling in my knapsack. "I don't have any money, but you can have this." I pulled out the Monkey King and dropped him on the table.

Sun stared at the brass monkey, dressed like a warrior, one leg raised as if plunging into battle, a spear poised for action. Sun picked him up and held him in his hands for a quiet moment.

"I remember this was your sister's favorite. Many times she played with him even when Tai-tai told her not to." He chuckled a bit, and I thought I saw tears in his eyes as he stroked the monkey's head. "Is the milk for your mother?" he asked softly.

"No, it's for Mei-mei. Mei-mei is very sick. Ma says you could help us. You would know where to get milk and limewater."

"Well, you are lucky. I can help you with that," Sun said looking relieved. He put the monkey down and said, "But it's too late today. We'll have to wait till tomorrow."

His wife came back into the room, and Sun added, "I bet you're hungry, Little Missy." This familiar term in Chinese didn't feel like me anymore. No one called me Little Missy anymore.

I hadn't eaten all day, and I wasn't sure how late it was, but I jumped up.

"I can't stay, Sun! I've got to get home tonight. I can't wait till tomorrow!"

His wife placed the bowl and chopsticks in front of Sun. Sun pushed them toward me.

"Do you think I'm going to let you go back out there alone? You don't want to return empty-handed, do you?"

"But—"

"It will be dark soon and, besides, I have some things to do before we leave."

Then suddenly I remembered the letter that Da had written. "Oh," I said, reaching inside my knapsack. "I forgot this. It's from Da."

"Ah," said Sun, taking the letter. "Well, you just sit down and eat while I read this. Then we can make a plan."

There before me was a steaming bowl of rice with cabbage and beans, pieces of chicken and garlic greens. The smell was overwhelming and drew me back into the chair. I had not smelled such a sweet aroma in so long. I stared at Sun in disbelief.

He laughed and said, "It's all right. My employer has connections. Now eat."

CHAPTER 23

un's wife nudged me awake the next morning. I had fallen asleep exhausted on a pallet she had rolled out for me. Just before I fell asleep, I felt for the dragonfly that was no longer around my neck, hoping Chiyoko held it as she fell asleep. Ma and Da would be worried sick if I did not return. I worried about Mei-mei. Isabella's song came to me: *"When at night I go to sleep . . ."* I couldn't remember all the words, but I hummed the tune and called to the angels.

"Oh, Mei-mei's angels," I prayed aloud, "please keep her safe until I get back."

I was up and ready in no time since I slept in my clothes. Sun was ready too, standing by the table and putting some things in a bag.

"I've arranged with my employer to be gone today. I need to prepare a few things in the kitchen upstairs before we go." He tied the bag and said, "Get your knapsack and come with me. We'll leave from upstairs."

I plodded behind Sun, up a narrow stairway to a storage room that led to the kitchen of the big house. Through the large window on the other side of the kitchen, I could see that the day was just breaking. There was enough light for Sun to move easily through the room, as if he knew every inch of it. Huge pots and pans hung from hooks over a long worktable in the middle of the room. Two large sinks were at one end. I just stood there while Sun bustled around, explaining that his wife would serve the family while he was gone.

He put some things I couldn't see in another bag and then led me through a swinging door into a room with cabinets full of dishes, and then out enormous double doors to a dining room with a long table and heavy chairs.

He pushed open a heavy sliding wooden door, which clapped together with a loud wooden sound when shutting. I was startled at the sound and afraid the noise would wake someone. Sun didn't seem concerned and kept moving.

I then found myself standing on marble squares of black and white. A curving staircase ascended on both sides of this enormous room. I stood in wonder. Even Auntie Boxin's house didn't have a grand entry like this.

I slid my feet along the shiny floors, trying to catch up with Sun, when a voice came from the top of the stairway.

"Sun, are you leaving now?" asked a well-spoken Chinese woman. She continued moving down the stairs as she talked. She was dressed in a blue silk robe tied at her waist with a matching belt. Her black hair was loose and fell softly over her shoulders.

"Is this the girl you told me about?" she asked when she got closer.

"Yes, this is the daughter of my former employer. I am taking her back home now."

"You used to work for the director of the water company, didn't you?" She was addressing Sun, but she put her hand on my chin and lifted my face into the light.

"Yes," Sun said.

"And his wife is American, isn't that right?"

She let go of my face, and I looked down. I noticed the sequined slippers sticking out from under her robe. How easy it would have been to stomp on her slippers and run, but instead I waited for Sun to answer. She went on.

"I studied in America. I went to school at Wesleyan College in

Macon, Georgia. Do you know it?"

I was startled to realize she was speaking English and addressing the question to me.

Not waiting for me to answer, she continued. "My English is rusty. I don't have anyone to speak to now. Perhaps you know someone who can teach me. I've been trying to think of a funny English expression, the one about saying something wrong, you know, something about your feet."

"You mean . . . putting your foot in your mouth?" I responded too quickly. Ma had taught me expressions like that.

"Yes, yes, that's the one. Putting your foot in your mouth. Thank you," she said, as if delighted.

My face flushed. *Is she trying to trick me, testing to see how well I speak English, to be sure I am the daughter of an American?* I wanted to correct myself, but it would have done no good.

The woman turned away and spoke directly to Sun in Chinese. "It is not safe for a young girl to be out alone. Take her safely home and stop by the merchant's and get what you need. Now be on your way."

"Yes, ma'am." Sun lowered his head in a polite bow.

Sun stopped at the merchant's as Madam Lu had instructed him. The seller seemed to be waiting for him and already knew what he wanted. He had things wrapped and in containers. While Sun began packing them into his bag, I looked around. Butchered ducks hanging from the ceiling. Sacks of rice and flour. Shelves of cans and jars. Onions, garlic . . . the smells of meat and herbs overwhelmed me.

And there in a bin were oranges. Oranges!

Not everyone has been eating moldy cornmeal!

"Come on," Sun said, when he was ready.

We walked quickly in the early morning light. Sun knew a way that avoided the barracks, and I made note of his route. When we arrived, I led him through the gate to our house.

Da opened the door. I could see the dark lines in his brow, but he didn't even ask what had happened. I was back and Sun was with me, and that was all that mattered.

"Welcome, Sun," he said. "Come in. We've been expecting you."

He told us that it had been a hard night for Mei-mei, and Ma had stayed with her all night.

Da told Sun to take the things he had brought to the kitchen. Amah turned her back when he came in and didn't speak to him. Sun was kind to her, put his things down, and told her he would be back in a minute. Da told him where Mei-mei was, and I led him to the bedroom. Both Ma and Mei-mei were asleep, side by side, with a thin blanket over them.

Sun walked over to the bed. Ma's eyes opened, but she didn't seem to recognize him until he spoke. When she heard his voice, a weak smile lit her face. Sun bent towards her and whispered something in her ear.

Ma smiled, "Nini must be with you."

Sun went back to the kitchen, and I stayed at Mei-mei's door, not venturing in as I'd been told. Ma got up. She stroked her hair back and tried to straighten the wrinkles from her clothes that she had slept in.

How different she must look to Sun, I thought. Her hair was gray and deep shadows lined her eyes. When she came towards the door and saw me, her face brightened further.

"Oh, Nini, she said. "Last night I thought I had lost you both, but something told me to hold on. I knew you would come. The worry just seeps out of me now."

Ma left the room before Sun came with warm milk. Mei-mei was awake then. Her legs moved restlessly. Sun sat beside her, speaking comforting words. Her legs calmed and her eyes opened. She seemed to float into awareness of Sun's presence. Sun coaxed her into sitting up and sipping the warm milk from a spoon he held.

"Now, Mei-mei, my girl, you have to get well. You know why? I have a surprise for you. I'll need your help. But you have to get well first."

Mei-mei didn't take her eyes off Sun's face as she sipped the milk silently.

I left them alone and went to find Da. I couldn't wait to tell him what Dr. Mori had said. I found him in the living room, but he was full of questions about Sun. When he had heard everything he wanted to know, I spoke.

"Da, I have some news from Dr. Mori."

"Dr. Mori? When did you see Dr. Mori?"

"Well, I—"

"Is that what took you so long?"

"I'm sorry, Da. You see—"

Before we could finish, Ma came into the room, and then Sun.

"You're a sight for sore eyes, indeed, Sun!" Ma spoke, her voice hoarse and dry. "My eyes have just gone to pieces. I didn't know who you were at first. Can't even read anymore. Sometimes the light just kills me."

"You are a pleasure for me to see too," replied Sun, not letting on what changes he must have seen in Ma or in any of us.

"Nini says you have a wife and baby," said Da.

"Yes, and another one on the way."

"I'm so happy for you! Tell us about your wife," Ma urged.

"She was the amah for the family that used to live in the house. Madame Lu kept her as a maid when she hired me as the cook."

"I've heard that Madame Lu is the mayor's sister." Ma broached the subject we all wanted to know.

"No, she's his sister-in-law, married to his brother. And she hates what the mayor is doing to the people. She hates all the collaborators," Sun huffed.

I was confused. "But why did you whisper in the garden? I thought you were scared that she would hear us."

"I don't trust the servants. Many of them used to work for the mayor." Sun had always been cautious around other servants.

I went on, letting out all my fears. "But she tricked me into speaking

English—and told you to take me home. I thought she only wanted to find out where we lived. Will she have Ma arrested?"

"No, no, she would never do that. When I told her I needed the day off, she began asking questions. When she understood the situation, she wanted to help you. She told me to go through the dining room and clang the doors shut so she'd hear us leaving and come down."

"You mean you planned it?"

"She wanted to meet you and see how you were. When she told me to get what I needed at the merchant's, I knew that was her way of saying that she approved of you, and she wanted to help."

I was too stunned to reply but thought, *Maybe I didn't put my foot in my mouth after all.*

"Well, Sun, if this war ends—" Da started.

"You mean, *when* it ends," Sun corrected.

"Yes, *when* it ends," Ma repeated. "Sun, we miss you. We hope you will come back when the war is over."

"That's what I wanted to tell you!" I burst out.

"What?" asked Ma.

"I went to see Chiyoko. I know I shouldn't have, but I found her message in the secret hiding place and I had to know if she was all right. Her family still lives over the clinic. Dr. Mori was there. He told me he heard at the hospital that Tokyo is being bombed, fires are breaking out everywhere. What do you think? Dr. Mori said it's not over yet but . . . what do you think?"

I spilled it out in one gush. They all looked at me stunned. I showed them the bottle of medicine from Dr. Mori and the tea Chiyoko gave me. The overwhelming news spared me from a scolding.

"I agree with Dr. Mori," said Da. "It's not over yet. "

"I'm so tired. I don't know if I can make it if it lasts much longer," Ma said.

"This is wonderful news, but things may not change quickly. We need to be cautious until we know more," Da warned.

Sun explained to Amah what to do with the things he had brought. She warmed up to him, at least enough to learn what she needed to do for Mei-mei.

When Sun finished, Da walked outside with him into the courtyard and to the gate.

For a moment, I felt good, that I had done something that helped. Sun had made my world seem normal again, but when he left, it all came crashing back around me. Everything was upside down. Sun, who was once our servant, was now taking care of us. Madame Lu, who I thought would betray us, was actually helping. Da refused to collaborate with the Japanese, yet those who had collaborated were well fed and could even get oranges. Ma had been hiding from the Japanese and now the news of the war ending still made everyone fearful. I was so confused and exhausted that I fell on the sofa without removing my shoes and slept.

CHAPTER 24

*T*hree days later, Sun returned. I saw him at our gate carrying many bundles. He wore black pants and a black shirt and had a pack on his back and something under his right arm. I ran and greeted him excitedly in Chinese.

"Mei-mei is better! Come see. She is sitting up now."

"That's good," he beamed. "How's your mother?"

"Not so good," I started, but noticed that the thing under his arm was wiggling. Sun came inside the gate and dropped the squirming bundle on the ground. A round ball of black and tan fur rolled out of his hands, and a Pekingese pup looked up at me with round, bright eyes.

"Do you think we can find him a new home?" Sun asked.

"Here?" I was stunned. We hadn't seen a pet since Sillibub.

"Oh, Sun!" I exclaimed and bent down to look at the little pup. His dark coat was thick and coarse, but his chest was soft and white. His heart-shaped ears were tan with little black tips. His face had a black mask extending across to the ears. He looked up at me, then nuzzled right into my legs. He had found a home.

"Do you think Mei-mei will get well for him?" asked Sun with a smile.

"I bet she will!" Then a dreadful thought came. "What will Amah say? We don't have enough food for us. She will never let us keep a pet."

"I've already thought of that too. I have some bones and meat scraps with me, and I'll bring more. Now, let's take the little fellow to meet his caretaker." Sun shifted the weight of his bag to the other shoulder, and we entered the house.

Mei-mei was sitting up in bed and grinned when Sun walked in the room. I stayed at the door and held the pup out of sight. Mei-mei obviously recognized Sun this time, but she didn't say anything. She was still weak and looked pitiful. Her hair was thin and wispy, and when Ma had tried to brush it, most of it had come out in the brush.

"Well, that's more like it," Sun said. "I'm glad to see you smiling. You need to keep getting better now. Do you think you can do that?"

Mei-mei smiled and nodded. Sun asked her to stick out her tongue. He held it and tugged on it a little to see how it looked and felt. Then he looked at her eyes and pulled down the skin below her eyes. "You look good to me," he said. Then he asked, "Are you able to take care of something for me?"

She spoke this time. "Yes, Sun. I'm much better now."

"I'm glad to hear it because this one needs you."

With that he motioned to me, and I let go, and the Pekinese pranced into the room. Sun picked him up and put him on Mei-mei's bed. The pup shook with joy as Mei-mei scooped him into her arms and hugged him.

Amah objected, just as I thought, but Sun spent some time alone with her in the kitchen and it was settled after he promised to bring the food. Even Ma and Da were willing to accept a pet if it meant seeing Sun more often.

Sun also had something for Ma. He went into the kitchen and soon came back with a bowl of hot dark liquid and handed it to Ma.

"Whew!" she said when she got a whiff of it. "It smells like something a donkey left behind."

Sun laughed. "It's liver tonic. I've been working on it for two days, boiling liver with herbs. It's good for your eyes and will give you energy too." He grinned.

Ma took a sip and scrunched her lips and squeezed her eyes together. "Anything that tastes this bad must be good for me, right? This is the first thing you've made that I didn't just gobble up."

Sun stood over her, watching to be sure she kept drinking it. "You have to get your strength back. As soon as you finish the whole bowl, I have some news for you."

Ma kept drinking but kept her eyes on Sun.

Has he heard something about the end of the war? I wondered. Maybe he had seen the airplanes!

Ma took the last sip and sighed with relief.

"Now, what's your news?"

Sun took the bowl from her and replied, "Nini told me you were teaching English."

"Yes, but I had to stop when Mei-mei got sick. And I haven't had the strength to start again."

"Well, you will have another student soon and she will pay handsomely for the service. She speaks English, but she wants to talk like you."

Is he talking about Madame Lu? I couldn't believe he would bring Madame Lu here!

"But—" I tried to warn Ma.

Sun went on. "She wants to start right away. What do you think?"

"You can't, Ma!" I blurted out. "You can't bring Madame Lu here."

"It's all right, Nini," said Sun.

Da spoke. "If she wanted to cause us harm, Nini, she would have already acted. I think we have to trust Sun."

"All right then," said Ma. "It is agreed—I will teach her. Thank you, Sun. Your news is just the tonic I needed."

When I walked with Sun to the door, he stopped and reached into his bag. "Here," he said. "You left this when you came to see me, but it belongs to you." He handed me something wrapped in cloth, but I knew what it was.

Time passed, but Madame Lu didn't come, not right away. I didn't realize how much I wanted her to come, for someone to come, something to happen. I was always waiting and wanting. Waiting for Madame Lu to come. Waiting for Zhao Ren to return. Wanting to see Chiyoko. Wanting to hear news that this war would end. I felt restless like Da.

One night I had a dream. I lay in a lush, green, grassy meadow looking up at a wide blue sky. A dragonfly landed on my forehead, then flew away. Others came, making no sound and not landing anywhere. I reached out to catch one, and they all vanished. Then I caught sight of one in the grass. I sat up and scooped the lone dragonfly in my hands. It was cut open right down the middle and inside was a shimmering jewel, sparkling like the rainbow. I reached for the jewel, and the whole thing disappeared.

CHAPTER 25

August 1945

The sky turned dark in the middle of the day. I was alone on the edge of the field, walking home, when I first heard a whirring in the distance. The sound grew louder and filled the air with a deafening beat. A line of darkness moved across the field as locusts filled the sky. Their brown wings and long legs, the little green eyes, buzzing, diving, were all around me. I swatted and swiped and ducked.

The locusts descended on the field, and in an instant the noise changed to a quieter, crunching sound. When they lifted again, the field lay bare. Not a blade of grass, not a weed or flower, not a shaft of wild millet remained—only bare, dry stalks stood like dying soldiers in a field of destruction.

Amazed and terrified, I ran home. Had anyone else witnessed it? Ma opened the door, a solemn and fearful look on her face.

"Where have you been, Nini? We've been looking for you."

"What is it?"

Just then Isabella came flying down the stairs. "Hurry, please. I need you. I don't think we have much time."

I followed Isabella up the stairs, Ma right behind me.

"Oh, Nini, I'm so glad you're here. Mother keeps saying your name. I think she wants to give you something."

Isabella rushed me to Auntie Boxin's room. Amah was by the bedside, talking quietly and gently patting down the blankets. Auntie Boxin lay against her pillows the way I had seen her so many times. Isabella took my hand and led me to her bedside. Auntie Boxin's eyes were shut.

"Mother, she's here . . . Nini's here."

Auntie Boxin's eyes opened, but she didn't speak. Her hand moved, and Isabella took my hand and moved it toward something Auntie Boxin was holding. I wanted to pull away fearing it was a bloody handkerchief, but I yielded to Isabella. She placed a leather bag in my hand.

I felt its weight in my palm. I opened the drawstring and saw inside the coins that Auntie Boxin had saved.

"She wanted to give you something for your kindness to her. I know these coins have no value now, but they were valuable to her, at least in her memory. She wanted you to have them. It's her way of thanking you."

Auntie Boxin lay still. Ma took Auntie Boxin's hand and felt the pulse, she stood there for a long silent moment, then Ma turned to Isabella and shook her head.

Isabella fell across the bed and sobbed, "Oh, no. Please wait, Mother. Please wait. What will happen to me? What will I do?"

Ma took Isabella in her arms and caressed her, while Amah gently folded Auntie Boxin's arms across her chest. Then she lifted the blanket and tucked it neatly around Auntie Boxin's shrunken body.

These coins, these useless coins! I was angry at Auntie Boxin. Why hadn't she waited a little longer? If she had waited, the war would end, and Dr. Mori would come. I didn't want her old coins! I felt guilty for being angry, for being gone so long, for hating to read to her, for yelling at her for hoarding flour. She had kept us alive with her rations, even her hoarded, moldy flour. I hated myself for abandoning her. All of it welled up inside of me. I felt sad and angry and guilty and afraid. I couldn't contain so many emotions at once.

I threw down the bag of coins and ran downstairs. I ran outside and through the gate. I ran across the barren, dry field as far as Amah had taken us the day we killed the snake.

There on the edge of the marsh, I stopped, panting and gasping for breath. A few green millet shoots poked their way through the dried mud. I grabbed the shoots in my hand and yanked them out of the ground. They disgusted me. I couldn't stand seeing one beautiful, peaceful, fresh green thing in all this destruction.

I was distraught and famished at the same time. My hunger took over and I bit and gnawed the ends of the green shoots, chewed and swallowed them in a furious rage. My stomach turned, repulsed by the bitter taste. I choked and gagged. My stomach turned inside out. All my anger and terror turning and knotting inside of me spewed out. I bent over the wasted field and vomited all that had happened to me that day, and all that had happened in those four long years.

Wiping my mouth, I stood. A dull sound buzzed in my head. I heard the buzzing from beyond the field. I looked up at the sky to the east. The buzzing grew louder.

In the sunlight, the airplanes were blue and green and silver—beautiful, shimmering and glorious. The planes flew in formation low over my head, their engines roaring.

I stood there alone, just me in the field on the edge of the marsh, watching the planes with the star on their wings flying overhead. I waved with the millet in my hand, hesitantly at first, then frantically. I dropped the shoots and ran toward home, hope shimmering like a jewel in my heart.

AUTHOR'S NOTE

*T*his book is based on the story of the Liu family. When I was just out of college and on my way to Japan to teach English, my Aunt Mary in California told me that her cousin Grace had married "a Chinaman" and moved to China with him years ago. China was closed at the time I learned this, but I set my heart on finding her one day. But, as it turned out, she found me.

Grace McCallie Divine (1901-1979), went to New York City from Chattanooga, Tennessee, to study music in 1928. There she met and married Liu Fu Chi, "F. C.," (1904-1955), a Chinese engineer who had just graduated from Cornell University and taken a job at New York's public works. They had a daughter named Ju-lan, whose nickname was "Nini." The Depression hit, and Mr. Liu returned to China to work for the water works in Tianjin. Grace and Ju-lan soon followed.

In 1937, the Japanese invaded mainland China, but the coastal cities had territories, called "concessions," owned and governed by European nations. The water works was located in the French Concession. Therefore, at first the Lius were shielded from the turmoil of the Japanese invasion. They had two more children, a daughter in 1937 and a son in 1941.

After the attack on Pearl Harbor, Japanese troops took control of the foreign concessions in China. The remaining Americans and Europeans were rounded up, forced to register as enemy aliens, and removed to internment camps until the end of the war.

Grace narrowly escaped internment for unknown reasons. She lived in hiding with the family until the war ended in August 1945. Her family back home did not know if Grace was alive until a Marine from Chattanooga, private Giles Brooks, found her, weighing barely eighty-six pounds, and sent word home that she had survived.

Grace Liu and her family continued to live in China after the war. Her husband died of lung cancer in 1955. Grace Liu taught English at Nankai University where she was arrested during the Cultural Revolution and accused of being a spy and counter revolutionary. After President Nixon and Chairman Mao established diplomatic relations between the two countries, she wrote to her family in Tennessee and returned in 1974 with her son, William. She had lived in China for forty years.

I had a chance to live with Grace the last year of her life and become very close to her. Her son William worked at UC Berkeley. Grace began to write her memories. With a diagnosis of cancer, her two daughters came from China to help with her care. This is the way I came to know my remarkable Chinese cousins. After Grace died in Berkeley in 1979, her two daughters returned to China where they both had families. William became the director of English language programs for Chinese interpreters at Simon Fraser University in Vancouver, Canada.

The full story is told in two books: *Grace in China: An American Woman Beyond the Great Wall, 1934*-1974 (Black Belt Press, 1999) and *Grace: An American Woman in China, 1934-74* (Soho Press, 2003) by Eleanor McCallie Cooper and William Liu.

In *Dragonfly Dreams*, the family (Chinese father, American mother, and three children) and the historical dates and facts form the structure of the story, like an envelope; but the content of the story, the letter that goes inside the envelope, is fictional.

PHOTOS

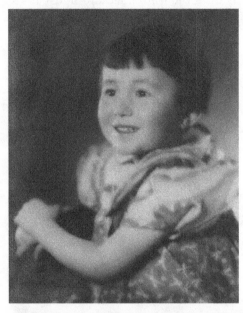

A photographer in Tianjin, China, captured the two sides of Ju-lan Liu as a child, dressed as an American girl and dressed as a Chinese girl.

F.C. Liu, holding his daughter Ju-lan, with their amah, Wang nai-nai, in Victoria Park, British Concession, Tianjin, China, 1935.

Ju-lan in 1942, age 10

Photo courtesy of Vivian Kwan

The Liu family, 1945.

From left: Ju-lan, Ellen, Grace, F.C. holding William. The photo was taken by Pvt. Giles Brooks, US Marine from Chattanooga, Tennessee, who sent word to Grace's family that she and her family had survived the war.

Passport picture of Grace McCallie Divine Liu with her three children, Ju-lan, William and Ellen, 1946. It was important for Americans with mixed-race children to be able to claim their children should they need to leave China. Grace never used this passport and did not return to the US until 1974 with her adult son William.

The three Liu children, William, Ju-lan, and Ellen, after the end of World War II. Ju-lan is holding their dog, Budgie. Photo was taken by US Marine Jimmy Lail from Chattanooga, 1946.

View of British Concession, Tianjin, China, during the Japanese bombing of the city of Tianjin, 1937. The Japanese did not take over the British Concession until after the bombing of the US Naval fleet in Pearl Harbor in 1941.

HISTORICAL TIMELINE

1842   First Opium War. Britain defeats China, gains treaty ports, called "concessions," in key coastal cities in China

1858   Second Opium War. European nations gain greater control of territories in China

1895   First Sino-Japanese War. Shifts power in Asia to Japan, led to Japanese occupation of Korea in 1910

1900   Boxer Rebellion. Anti-foreign rebellion in China was defeated by Britain, France, Russia, Japan, Germany, Italy, Austria, and the US, forcing China to pay indemnity

1908   Indemnity Scholars. US returned the remainder of the Boxer indemnity payments ($17 million) as scholarships for Chinese students to study in the US

1937   Japan invades China, takes control of coastal cities, except for the concessions under European control in those cities*

1939 Germany invades Poland
Britain and France declare war on Germany

1940 Tripartite Pact between the Axis Powers: Germany, Italy, and Japan

1941 Japan attacks Pearl Harbor, takes control of European concessions in China
US declares war on Japan
Nazi Germany declares war on US

1942 Nazis deported Jews to concentration camps
Japan deported Westerners in China to internment camps

1945 Germany surrenders May 1945
US burns Tokyo, drops atomic bomb on
Hiroshima and Nagasaki
Japan surrenders August 1945**

* Britain, France, and other European countries had established territories in China. When Japan occupied China in 1937, Japanese troops did not move into these foreign-held territories, waiting until after the start of war in Europe and the bombing of Pearl Harbor. After December 1941, the Europeans remaining in these territories were forced to register and were sent to internment camps until the end of the war.

**The occupation of China by Imperial Japan required enormous numbers of troops and civilians to support the troops. Dr. Mori is a fictional character who represents one of those civilians.

AUTHOR'S BIO

*E*leanor McCallie Cooper is drawn by her deep roots in the South to stories that have been hidden or forgotten. She captures her own family stories on the edge of traumatic historical events that portend personal and social turmoil.

She co-authored, with William Liu, *Grace in China: An American Woman Beyond the Great Wall,* (Black Belt Press, 1999) and *Grace: An American Woman in China, 1934-74,* (republished by Soho Press in 2003). The Chinese translation was published by SDX Joint Publishing Company in 2006.

Before taking up writing, Eleanor worked for non-profits both in California and Tennessee, addressing community and social issues. She has been a consultant for civic engagement and community-wide visioning. Eleanor earned a doctorate in education from the University of Tennessee at Chattanooga with a focus on community learning and leadership.

Eleanor lived in Japan for two years, taught English at Kinjo University, and was a guide for the US pavilion at the World's Fair, Expo '70, in Osaka. Leaving Japan, she traveled around the world by herself. She has traveled extensively in Korea, China, India, and many places in Europe.

She lived in New York and San Francisco before returning to her home town of Chattanooga, Tennessee, where she now lives with her husband and family.

STUDY GUIDE

Questions for classroom or group discussion:

1. Why does Nini feel that the foreign girls at school treat her as if she is the foreigner in China?

2. It's easy to identify with Ma's confusion about how a small island nation could occupy a large country like China. Why do you think Japan waited until the bombing of Pearl Harbor to take over the foreign-controlled areas in China?

3. What do oranges and airplanes represent in Nini's imagination? What do snakes and frogs represent? Along this same line, why did Sun give a puppy to Mei-mei?

4. When Nini was quarantined with the whopping cough, she felt like all of China was quarantined from the rest of the world. Can you describe your feelings during the Covid-19 pandemic?

5. What do you think happened to Chiyoko after the war?

6. In this story, there are many examples of the need for one person to forgive another person. Name those you can think of. Why is the theme of forgiveness important to war?

7. In the story, the principal at Nini's school blamed America for China's troubles and compared Americans to devils who wanted to "chop off children's heads." Nini knew this was not true, and yet she was still treated badly. Later she learned about *propaganda*. Today we hear people blame China for causing America's problems. How can you distinguish between what is true and what is not?